Happy Holidays!

Happy Holidays!

Prateek Surana

PARTRIDGE
A Penguin Random House Company

Copyright © 2015 by Prateek Surana.

ISBN: Hardcover   978-1-4828-5691-0
           Softcover   978-1-4828-5690-3
           eBook   978-1-4828-5689-7

All rights reserved. No part of this book may be used or reproduced by any means, graphic, electronic, or mechanical, including photocopying, recording, taping or by any information storage retrieval system without the written permission of the author except in the case of brief quotations embodied in critical articles and reviews.

Because of the dynamic nature of the Internet, any web addresses or links contained in this book may have changed since publication and may no longer be valid. The views expressed in this work are solely those of the author and do not necessarily reflect the views of the publisher, and the publisher hereby disclaims any responsibility for them.

Print information available on the last page.

To order additional copies of this book, contact
Partridge India
000 800 10062 62
orders.india@partridgepublishing.com

www.partridgepublishing.com/india

Preface

*"Some memories in our lives become a
part of us yet aren't ever spoken of. These
moments of impact prove potential for change
in the way we think and the way we live.
It has ripple effects far beyond what we
can predict-Reuniting some people after
ages and making them closer than before,
while sending others spinning off into great
ventures- Landing them where they would
never have thought to have found themselves.
That's the thing about memories like these.
No matter how hard we try to control them,
they keep flashing in our heads, pioneering
the way we think and the way we speak.
These moments of impact will perhaps never
return in our lives yet our souls feed on
them. The moments which now seem like a
long lost vacation- The Happy Holidays..."*

Chapter 1

Happy Holiday Begins!

"If I speak in the tongues of men or of angels, but do not have love, I am only a resounding gong or a clanging cymbal. If I have the gift of prophecy and can fathom all mysteries and all knowledge, and if I have a faith that can move mountains, but do not have love, I am nothing. If I give all I possess to the poor and give over my body to hardship that I may boast, but do not have love, I gain nothing.

Love is patient, love is kind. It does not envy, it does not boast, it is not proud. It does not dishonor others, it is not self-seeking, it is not easily angered, and it keeps no record of wrongs. Love does not delight in evil but rejoices with the truth. It always protects, always trusts, always hopes, and always perseveres.

Love never fails. But where there are prophecies, they will cease; where there are tongues; they will be stilled; where there is knowledge, it will pass away. For we know in part and we prophecy in part, but when completeness comes, what is in part disappears. When I was a child, I talked like a child; I thought like a child, I reasoned like a child. When I became a man, I put the ways of childhood behind me. For now we see only a reflection as in a mirror; then we shall see face to face. Now I know in part; then I shall know just as I am fully known.

And now these three remain: faith, hope and love. But the greatest of these is love."

-The Holy Bible

November indeed had been bringing in a sense of frostiness in its breeze, tincturing the being of a man who was lost in his train of thoughts...

The Celsius Scale at Bhimtal had taken a considerable dip making it one of the coldest nights in the fall of 2010.

This time- last year; things were completely different.

Perhaps- Like a fairy tale!

Two best of friends would've been complete strangers if it hadn't had been 2010 that brought them to this predicament.

There would've been no grand Indian wedding to attend to and no wedding preparations to keep everyone busy...

But things did change and with each deafening touch of the wind Rohit rekindled a part of him that had been lost for long.

After having burnt a baffling amount of calories on the dance floor, Adarsh was left with no energy to question Rohit's vacant stare into emptiness!

He stretched himself on one of the two rocking chairs that were placed in the balcony of their hotel room which gave a view of a beautiful lake that was located at the rear of the Hotel Neelesh Inn.

Sunrise wasn't far away.

Very soon it was going to be beginning of the day when the first amongst the five peers got married!

Woolgathering the moment's peace Rohit kept gazing for some more time and then…

After a period of brief silence, the long lost part of his being resurrected itself:

"I've always wondered how different things could've been if I had reacted differently.

Whatever has been the outcome, I am the sole person to be held responsible for it! It's completely my fault. I have ruined everything.

I hate myself and my bloody mouth!"

The all of a sudden outburst took Adarsh by surprise.

At first, he stammered to get hold of what he actually wanted to speak.

But once the words were chosen, he prepared his questionnaire in no time!

"Could you stop acting weird and tell me what's going on?

I'm feeling really awkward sitting next to you and not having any clue as to what you are talking of!

What is it that has been keeping you upset?"

Rohit kept a wry smile on his face and continued...

"I am sorry but there's this thing about which I should've let you know, yet, I've kept it a secret from all of you.

There's this girl whom I love..."

...And before he could continue any further, Adarsh rose from his chair, startled at Rohit's words, with his mouth wide open.

Adarsh *(oozing with astonishment)*: "Don't tell me that you're in a relationship!!!

If my best friend has been in a relationship; with my having no clue about it I'll be heartbroken!

Please tell me, what I think; I'm expecting isn't true!

Wasn't I trustworthy enough that you've kept it a secret from me?"

Rohit *(calming Adarsh with his gestures)*: "Hush… Not at all bro!

Nothing's like that.

I have always had complete faith in you and that is the very reason I'm sharing with you now, what has been trapped inside me for quite some time.

Even Abhay and Karan aren't aware of it.

You're the first person to whom I'm talking to regarding this!

But before he could go any further, Abhay and Karan entered the room after having exhausted themselves on the dance floor of the still going on bachelor's party in the hotel premises.

On seeing them, Rohit stopped at where he was, but, Adarsh robustly went on to exclaim as if it was an entrance speech:

"Rohit is in a relationship!"

Rohit, continuing from where Adarsh finished:

"…And this is exactly why I was hesitant in the first place!

…Douche bag!"

This seemed to have swiped away the smiles from their faces turning it into a look of profound anxiety.

A million questions appeared on everybody's faces as they kept staring at Rohit's vignettes.

Rohit, on the other hand, had lost complete track of the scheme of events and started stammering before he could complete unveiling one of the secrets of his life.

An episode of swearing filled the room and after a session of cursing Abhay and Karan in their own ways ended up asking the same questions over and over again…

Karan-"Who is she?"

Abhay-"Why haven't you told us about her?"

Karan-"Bunk all those issues… what I'm interested in knowing, is that, how could a nerd like you end up in finding yourself a real girl!"

Abhay-"I bet it's that horny b**** who had been hitting on him…"

Adarsh-"LOL- What non-sense… Who is this horny b****?"

Karan-"Hasn't he told you about her?

There was this girl who had been hitting on him just the day after she saw him give a presentation at the conference he had to attend last week!"

Adarsh-"Crap! Is this true Rohit?"

Rohit-"Dude!"

"Don't dude me! Is this true?"

"...a bit of it but!"

"...Rohit! I'm a complete stranger to all of it...!

Why didn't you tell me about her?"

Rohit looked bemused.

"Well... There wasn't actually anything that was worth telling buddy!

She wasn't worth talking of!

Quite often she would buzz me late at night and then start with those lousy chats stating how much she liked me and what she had been wearing and..."

"What crap...!?

Are you serious?

...And... How come these kinds of girls get acquainted to you in the first place?

Why am I the unlucky one?

You could've given her my number... I'm very much available"

There was this hint of a smile on Rohit's face but, he made sure that he hadn't given it away.

He was aware of the backslapping which was pretty common in his friend circle. However, he was in no mood to be awarded with one of them which would make his back burn the entire night!

Therefore, somehow; he managed to hide his smile and continued:

"I never wanted to indulge myself in those filthy conversations buddy! Neither would I want my brother to do so... You know pretty well... I'm not of that kind!

She was perhaps doing all that because of my money or because of her lust; and I seriously hate such people from the bottom of my heart.

Do you really expect me to fall for such people?

She wasn't the one and if it means anything to you, then I'm sorry for not having told you anything about it.

The story behind the one who actually mattered goes way back to the time when I had started working..."

...And before Rohit could speak any further, Adarsh slammed him on his back in the exact manner, which Rohit had feared.

"...Bloody hell Rohit!

All of this has been going on since then and I wasn't even aware of it!

This is preposterous!

You are so dead buddy!

Call up auntie and tell her that, you won't be returning home anymore!"

Rohit *(trying to rub his back against the wall in an attempt to assuage the pain)*: "Aaaggh! You stupid moron!

At least let me complete what I have to say!

Do anything that you wanna do, but at least have the patience to allow me narrate..."

Karan *(interrupting)*: "All right, All right!

Both of you....calm down!

Go ahead and finish your story Rohit.

I'll make sure that you remain alive till that time...

I need to know the exact reason as to why your kindergarten friends were kept strangers to it!

... and it better be a good one"

Rohit *(resting himself on the side table and crouching his legs in a manner that could protect his face and upper torso in the event of another backslap):* "Alright!

I'm starting at inception so that you may know everything that's worth knowing!

... Our family business had been going on in the form of a HUF for a very long time. I wanted to get it converted into a Private Limited Company and for this issue I had approached my Chartered Accountant so that he could help me with the entire procedure.

Things were on track and looked great!

But then all those leading compliances were becoming a big headache so I approached the same firm once again and asked the managing partner o'er there if he could delegate somebody who could help me out with the secretarial compliances!

... And he did send an intern who was competent enough for the job and that was how we met the first time.

However, once the incorporation activities were complete, I actually started missing her presence in my office.

But, I classified that as a normal feeling which a man might have when he's attracted to a girl whom he had been meeting on a regular basis.

Business doesn't look into feelings!

So, I ignored those feelings and things were quite normal...

Yet, all of this was only until I realized that my favorite cafeteria was the one which was regularly visited by her as well!

We bumped into each other quite often o'er there...

It had become almost certain that we would get to see each other over there during lunch hours.

This is how all of it was given a new beginning ...

Saying this, Rohit gave way to a brief period of silence!

Abhay *(Abruptly breaking the silence)*: "What next?

Bro, we need to know everything!

If you are thinking that by simply telling us the story of how you people met- you're gonna get away; then you're wrong.

So please E-LA-BO-RATE!!!"

Rohit *(taking a deep sigh)*: "Well, how do I explain the entire episode? I had no freaking idea as to how all of this had happened. It was perhaps only when I had realized that..."

Abhay: "Only when what?"

Rohit seemed frustrated...

He rolled up his sleeves and then unfolded them and kept repeating the same act over and over.

Then he took out his cell phone and started scrolling up and down his phonebook and then locked his screen and continued doing that for some time.

Adarsh *(taking away his phone)*: "What's her name?"

Rohit went blank again. He had a very curious look on his face.

Something highlighted the confusion on his mind that he had wanted to go on with the narration but, at the same time; he didn't want himself to be reminded of the incidents that had taken place in his life.

Abhay-"Don't commove us by narrating incomplete episodes from your life, Rohit!

Whatever it is... Speak out!"

Rohit: "Let her name be untold bro.

I'll tell you the entire story but let her name be untold.

I don't want you guys to know her.

There are certain reasons because of which I have sworn not to take her name... so... I hope you can understand what I mean!"

Karan: "Boss, don't you trust us or what?

What harm will it do if you mention her name?

It's going to remain only amongst the four of us."

Rohit: "I'm sorry bro but that can't happen...I simply can't mention her name.

If you want to know everything then you will have to comply with this only condition of mine that, I have placed in front of you."

Karan: "What the heck! Alright, just tell us your story."

Rohit: "At first I was a bit hesitant about going and talking to her while she was with her friends. But then, I found out a few work related issues as a conversation starter to get things going.

Though this took some time, I became well conversant with her and her work friends as well.

We guys went out in groups for some time and then, not because of any specific reason both of us started liking spending time alone in each other's company.

Initially these one to one meetings were due to the reason of our planning a surprise birthday party of our common friends or something of that sort.

But, slowly there were no reasons that could have been assigned to our meetings.

There were persistent durations of silence in these get-togethers.

However, we still liked sitting next to each other and casually talked about our daily happenings.

It was a bit awkward at first but, somehow conversations did start and one thing would always lead to another. We never realized how time would fly!

Her nagging boss was perhaps a common small talk which entertained her the most but, as we spent more time with each other we started rejoicing each other's company even more.

We started knowing each other's likes and dislikes and those were perhaps the best moments of our day!

But there was this one thing which always worried her whenever we were to meet:

Her parents would become livid whenever she spoke of hanging out with a guy friend of hers'.

As a matter of fact, it was; as if she had committed a sin.

She always told me that her parents were very conservative and hanging out alone with a male friend of hers' was something that was considered as a social crime.

Society always raises questions on women who are too independent or liberal in their lifestyle.

You just can't wave a magic wand and change the society you live in... Can you?

None of her sisters, including her, were given the permission to hang out alone with any of their male friends unless they met in groups.

The reason for these restrictions was that her parents were firm believers of the ways of the society they lived in.

According to these so called customs; whenever two people of the opposite sex are found to be alone in each other's company, people start making stories about them and her parents wanted to avoid all these social small talks.

Her father, in particular, had firmly ingrained in his mind that none of his daughters did anything that would destroy the set of principles he diligently followed.

He was very strict in his ways and for this very reason, she always feared to open her heart out in front of him.

But, truth be told, it wasn't only me who didn't want her to follow the rules that her parents had laid down.

I mean, we were simply two very good friends who liked talking a lot to each other and sharing stuff; which we didn't find comfortable enough in sharing with anybody else. And therefore, our meetings with each other in solitude became an act of denigration in the eyes of her parents.

It wasn't as if we were dating but...

...thus for these reasons, even she avoided telling her parents that she had been meeting me.

We never felt anything for each other to be awkward, even when meeting each other had become a daily ritual.

It wasn't as if we were in love or something, but; simply because our workplaces were very close and talking our hearts out was perhaps something that we both needed.

My daily schedules were literally planned in such a way so that I could manage to make sufficient time to meet her.

I don't know why, but, whatever time I could manage; always seemed less.

I'm sorry to say this, but, many a time, I had to avoid you guys in particular and bunk a lot of other official and family meetings just so that I could be with her.

Abhay- "Assh***"

Karan- "This is exactly what I hate with people falling in love... You guys tend to disregard everything else that exists in the world.

Oh! I'm dearly waiting for your story to end Rohit. Now, even I've teamed up with Adarsh for smashing your face against the wall, once you are done with your narration."

There were a few smiles and a few swears.

The seriousness that was creeping up had perhaps been let loose with the descriptions that Rohit gave way to.

An unexplained reason of prosperity shimmered on Rohit's face; which however, was a guest for only a few moments.

Somewhere at the back of his mind, there was something untold, which filched away his smile and he thought that it would be better that he continued his narration without any further delay.

In my defense, all I can say is that, we weren't in love with each other at that point in time.

We were simply two individuals of the opposite sexes; who had happened to get along pretty well.

However, as intimate friendship between people from opposite sexes is something that is questioned a lot in society, her parents always kept a check on her meeting any of her male friends; particularly me!

So, one of the first things that I had also learnt being with her was that, my spending time with her in isolation was a topic that was never to be discussed at her home.

We were best buds and..."

Adarsh *(interrupting Rohit before he could continue any further):* "Is she Pragya?"

Rohit: "I guess I've made it pretty clear that I am not going to take her name.

You may make as many assumptions as you want to, but, I am simply not going to take her name... Period!

Managing both -work and studies, is a very challenging job for those undergoing internship. The pressure of her upcoming exams had been taking a toll on her lifestyle.

Therefore, she decided to take leave from work so that she could sit down and focus on her academics.

...you guys must be aware of the fact as to how people go into hibernation mode once they are on an examination leave. Similar to theirs' was her situation.

With only three months left to her examination and her house being outside the perimeters of the city, meeting each other itself became a big challenge."

Abhay: "Are you nuts? Just because she was going on leave didn't mean that you guys couldn't meet each other.

I mean, on one end, you're talking of meeting her as a daily ritual and the very next moment you are making a contradictory statement of deciding not to meet her for three straight months.

Were you two supposed to meet each other only when she was at work?

I mean, you could've easily met each other someplace else even when she was on leave!

She could have come up midway somewhere and both of you could...

Suddenly Abhay realized that given the family situation that was just described, finding a reason to leave home would've been really difficult for her.

He knew he wasn't being correct yet, since he had to complete his sentence he quickly modified his words and continued to go on:

I am not going to buy this excuse as a reason which stopped you from meeting her for three straight months.

You could've travelled to meet her if she was that special for you!

No wonder the frequency of your conversations with me increased near about those examinations!

When she was busy with her exams, and you needed a friend to talk to- you started pinging me!

You bloody opportunist!"

Adarsh *(Affirming Abhay)*: "You're lucky you got away with one whack!

I feel like….Aaaggh!

You….. Do you think that we are fools who'll accept this story of yours?

…please don't make up this crappy version!"

Rohit: "…in the name of god!

Will you people let me complete before coming to these baseless conclusions!

Making her sacrifice some valuable time pre exams didn't seem like a feasible option at that time.

I am supposed to be her well-wisher and not her time killer!

But FYI, we did meet after she had been on leave, but could you please have the patience to allow me to come to that point!

If you guys don't know what I've been through, at least stop guessing!"

Karan: "Alright sir! Sorry for stopping you. You may proceed!"

Rohit: "Once she was on leave, finding a reason to leave home was something in which she found great difficulty.

Both of us were very eager to see each other! Somehow, after putting in a lot of thinking we devised a plan that allowed her to meet me at a coffee shop close to her house.

We were literally like two caged birds who had felt the vastness and the freshness of the sky after an eternity of captivity.

The only difference between the two of us was that, where, on one hand, her house was where she had been caged, the entire world seemed like a prison with me not getting to meet her.

She had managed very little time and both of us had a lot to talk of.

I had no clue as to where I should begin blabbing so I thought that a simple 'hi' would suffice the need of a conversation starter.

This was then followed by the general small talk!

She reciprocated some of my questions and then, without our even realizing, we were lost in each other's words....

She seemed tensed but, never admitted it...

When I tried inquiring about it, she would seem to dodge my questions by counter-questioning me.

Then suddenly, she brought up this topic that, once she was over with her studies, her parents, who had been looking for a guy, would get her married immediately.

All, which she had asked for, was a bit more time so that she could achieve something professionally.

But, to this, her father would always reply that profession is something that can be pursued even after marriage, and as she was the eldest amongst his four daughters, he didn't find it good enough to delay her marriage as he had to cater to the responsibility of his other daughters as well...

I don't know why; but; as soon as she raised this issue, I became very nervous!

I didn't have an explanation to this sudden nervousness of mine.

I mean, she was only 23. When I was of her age; marriage was something completely out of the question.

I had never been confronted to the situation to which she had been confronted to when I was of her age.

Was this because I am a boy and coz she is a girl?

Sometimes, things are taken for granted!

At 23 I was certain that I had ample time to settle down in life before I could even consider marriage. And no one questioned me for this delay! It was a correct decision by a man of my age... that's how the masses would state.

But, I never realized the fact that it was something which would affect my best friend this deeply!

I had no clue, that simply because she was a girl, society, in its own way, had started questioning her age and her not being married away by her parents!

Aren't we people of the modern era?

In today's world, where there has been a dramatic change in the way people think, I was seriously amazed to discover that there are some people who withhold the prophecies of yesteryears till date.

Is finding a life partner everything when there are women who want to exceed in the professional fields?

Till date the sex roles are almost predetermined... Men belong to the offices and women to the kitchen!

Pink is for girls and blue is for boys!

I was angry with all these thoughts coming into my mind yet my hands were tied. I was a complete no one to act on the situation!

She kept on telling me that a marriage proposal had come from Bangalore which was under serious consideration by her parents, out of the many proposals that they had been getting for her; since she had turned 20."

Karan- "...Mother of God! ...Isn't that a bit too early?"

Rohit-"At first, even I thought so.

You and I, we live in the heart of a metropolitan city! Try visiting the outskirts... People have a philosophy that the sooner their daughter is married the better it will be.

It is indeed very hard to believe if we place ourselves in the center of the city but, can be easily thought of once we start travelling.

Taking into consideration the interests in being independent; that have come up nowadays, I failed to understand why marriage is something that has kept bowing down women whenever the age bar set for them had been attained!"

Adarsh- "I... I hate to say this...

But I've got a gut feeling that it's P...."

Ah never mind!!!

Continue….."

Rohit- "… Thanks!

(Continuing) She wasn't happy with the way things were happening at her home.

Somewhere, she kept cursing the way things were meant to be but, somewhere, she always found an answer to all of it in her feminism.

Deep inside her heart, she had accepted that, even though she didn't like the fact that, she wouldn't be given many opportunities to pursue her career lest she got married into a family which allowed her to do so; it was something which she would have to live with, being a girl of her age born into the society of which she was a part.

She kept expressing her unwillingness to leave the city and how she would miss everything in the city where she had been born and brought up.

She expressed care for her parents for when they would turn old!

But, every time she raised this issue, she almost spontaneously sighed and consoled herself by making her womanhood a prime excuse for her situation!

I pictured the entire scenario almost impromptu.

A life which crippled me from expressing the state of my heart to her was something that was way too uncomfortable for my liking.

She had become my best friend within a very short span of time and I simply couldn't allow myself to accept the fact that I would have to distance myself from her in the very near future.

So, out of nowhere I asked:

"What about me as a husband?"

She had been expecting a more serious answer from me. But when she heard my reaction, she started laughing.

Her snow white face turned pink as she tried to gasp some air to catch a breath.

I had never intended to crack a joke and yet she felt that I was kidding with her just to make her feel good.

"Rohit- you really have a good sense of humor.

For a moment I literally felt that you were making a proposal."

Truth be told, I had no freaking idea as to what on earth was I talking about.

I mean, I had never planned to speak of anything of this sort.

It was completely momentary and I had given it absolutely no thought before the words just flowed out of my mouth!

I was numb... shit scared!

I could literally hear the sound of my thumping heart as if it were a ringing bell in a nearby temple.

My hands were literally shaking while I simply gazed into the innocence of her laughter, which made me more hesitant to the words that I chose to speak in front of her.

She responded to my so called joke with a flawless smile and passed it on as if it were just another daily blue...

"You and I would make a great pair...

I mean, we know each other so well that spending our lives with each other would be so much fun.

We would keep talking for hours and hours...

But, alas... this is something on which I can't take a call!

You would have to undergo my parents' approval for that to have happened."

"Why?

Are they the one's who'll be marrying me or will it be you?"

Suddenly there was a sputter of unexpected laughter which was meant to be an immediate answer to my question:

"...Hahaha! Grow up Rohit!

How can I take a decision on such issues?

Of course it'll be mamma-papa who will make the call.

That's how it goes!"

I faked a smile to her reply.

Of course her parents' consent was necessary but, couldn't she simply express her opinion!!

This and many other similar things kept going in and out of my mind.

...There were conflicting thoughts in my mind to the answer I got from her.

One part of my mind resisted me to give her further explanations and pass on the entire affair as a joke.

The other part, however, insisted me to go on and elaborate things further so that I could explain to her that I wasn't joking at all.

There was a moment's pause before I could actually end up committing myself to one of these two contradicting thoughts that were occupying my mind at that moment.

Once the thinking was done, I made a ho-hum start to unfold my mentation further:

"So... If my parents sent my marriage proposal to your parents; would you marry me??"

To be honest with you guys, I really wanted her to make a call at that time!

She stood right in front of me waiting for each and every word that I had spoken of, to sink in her heart.

I was quite confident on what I had said even though I wasn't sure why I had said so.

I had started anticipating her answer to be a positive one but, I was literally pissed off to know that she was nothing but defunct when it came to taking such an important decision of her own life.

I agree that parents do play a significant role in deciding whom their daughters are to be married to but, it obviously doesn't imply that a girl can't even think of choosing a guy of her liking!

Aren't arranged marriages supposed to be a system where the parents set up their children on a date; or what?

Shouldn't parents be more open to their children so that they can actually feel free to have a discussion on their likes and dislikes?

The concept of arranged marriages in the general society is such that marriage proposals are sent to the bride's/groom's family and they; after evaluating the proposer's family background and the worthiness of the proposer decide if it is worth being accepted or not.

This concept has been in practice for a long time, and on numerous occasions, even though the individuals have their own say on such decisions, no one ever objects the involvement of their entire family.

Sometimes, it is associated with prudence to take the advice of the elderly but, mostly these decisions are overshadowed and imposed with convincing and practical speeches.

Abhay- "Oh yes... The elated crap!

Any who, what did you do after this!"

Rohit gulped down his frustration and stared at the inquisitiveness that had come on the faces of his friends.

Not knowing what to say next, he thought it was better to unfold the incomplete episode of his life, rather than sharing how he had actually felt about the entire affair.

Thus, curbing his unexpressed emotions; he continued:

"Her laughter stopped...

She looked at me right in the eye and my eyes... well...they started flickering as I tried doing the same.

For a moment they stared at the seriousness that had suddenly come up on her face and then, at the very next moment I found myself looking at her feet.

"Are you serious?"

I kept smiling. But, only I knew of the big bang that had been taking place inside me.

I nodded my head in affirmation but didn't utter a word.

Abhay-"Hahaha! Fraidy-cat!!!! At least you could've gone on to say yes!"

Rohit-"Abhay will you please shut up, else I'll literally bang your head against this very wall to make you stop talking!

You are bugging me big time!

It's always easier said than done!

You're the one who's afraid of talking to girls... And look... who's giving me the expert advice!

...Perhaps I can never explain how difficult it was for me to express my emotions in front of her!

You ought to understand it only when you're put under similar circumstances!

Abhay- "Well... What if I tell you that I've been through these emotions?"

Rohit, Karan & Adarsh *(shouting together):* "What!"

Abhay- ".... Hahaha! Just kidding! You should have seen the look on your faces!"

There was a distinct period of silence.

Rohit raged like a bull before inviting a moment's peace to his self-portrayal.

After having sighed, he went on with this business:

She kept staring at me and then suddenly rose up and left.

I remained mum and didn't intend on speaking any further as she left the café.

I was too pensive to speak of anything else. All I did was waiting for an answer, which I didn't get at that time.

She simply rushed out without even caring to turn and show her face.

As she did, her hair brushed my face blackening the last expression that she gave way to.

I wanted to gaze into her eyes to let her know how true I was with what I had said, but, only if she could've turned back!

I wasn't comfortable with her leaving me in disarray without providing me with an answer.

But, what else could I have done!

The best thing which I could do to express myself had already been done; so; I had absolutely no clue as to what could be done next!

I sat there like a dodo and reacted very blankly to whatever that was happening around me.

Nothing else came to my mind except for the fact that I had actually asked her to marry me.

I had never planned anything of that sort!

...Thinking of her was the only thing that my mind could have possibly done at that time.

It had perhaps forgotten that I existed.

My heart; my soul; everything seemed lifeless as I pondered on her absence.

A million questions came up:

I hope she's alright!

I hope she understands that I was serious.

What if she takes it as a joke?

I'll tell her that I was joking if she starts making fun of me!

Will she make fun of me?

Will she call?

Will she text?

Should I call?

Should I text?

Nah... She'll think that I'm desperate

I think I should play the waiting game!

Hmm...That'll be good!

But, should I wait?

Even though none of the questions relating to her bugged me for long, she was the only thing which I kept thinking of!

Later when I reached home I received a text from her.

It contained only two words: "Why Me?"

I didn't have a reply to it.

I texted back if it would be appropriate for me to give her a call!

There was no reply from her end for the next two minutes.

Even two minutes seemed to break me apart at that moment.

I was extremely impatient!

So, I decided to end the waiting game by calling her but she disconnected my call on the very first ring.

I couldn't understand the reason.

Perhaps it was a mistake at her end! So I decided on calling her again!

...The same act repeated!

This made me clear that she didn't want to talk to me o'er the phone.

I waited and waited for a reply and after a deluded delay she finally texted back saying that she didn't feel it to be comfortable enough to talk o'er the phone at that hour.

She preferred dealing the entire affair by chatting o'er what's app!

My fingers were literally glued to my cellphone at that time and I kept staring at it; waiting for it to buzz at that point in time...

And my wait wasn't for long...

The first ring was like a gong which made me feel as if my examination results were out!

I didn't know what it had in store for me and simply hoped that whatever it was, it brought nothing but good news!

"Are you serious?"

I wanted to know how she kept feeling at each and every moment while we conversed via texts.

I tried using all sort of emoticons but nothing actually proved to be helpful at that time!

To be honest, I really dislike the concept of people conversing over texts.

More so, after this incident!

Yes- It's nice given under certain circumstances, but the fact needs to be accepted that people are losing the art of talking to each other with the increasing use of chatting via text messages.

I mean what on earth had she been expecting from me; as an answer to that message of hers'!

Of course I was damn serious about everything, else why would I have gone on to propose her indirectly for the second time!

I wanted to talk to her but...

I failed to understand how I could converse on such an issue by texting! At that time, I realized that text chats are nothing but a mere sham to factual conversations.

People are losing the art of vocation with the increasing usage of text messages!

Leave aside talking o'er the phone- two people sitting next to each other; have their minds hovering o'er some other place appreciating to chat with someone in the other end of the world rather that cherishing the company they have.

Facebook and What's app have become more of an addiction than a utility!

The Short Messaging Service is slowly turning into the Sole Messaging Service!

...I badly needed to express myself vocally at that time, but I had no other option other than texting her!

I failed to express how deeply my sub-conscious mind had been talking to me throughout all this and regarding what I had spoken to her throughout the entire day.

I told her to relax and not to get tensed.

But, honestly speaking, that was something, I guess, I had been consoling myself with.

I went on to tell her that I had always learnt to express myself and that there weren't any two faces of mine.

I had a feeling in my heart which I had shared with her and I expected her to give me a genuine reply; without it being prejudicial to our friendship!

…There was no reply from her end.

I kept texting her over and over again but there was no reply. So, I asked her if she could confirm her receiving all the messages…

She texted in affirmation!

I mean, I sent her around 40-50 texts and all I got was a single 'Ya!' in turn!

WTF!

At least she could've put in some more effort by typing a few more letters!

…My mind started making all sorts of permutations and combinations.

Has she gone off to sleep?

Is she awake?

Is she thinking about me?

What else could she be thinking of?

How would she be feeling?

Will it be a yes?

Will she reject me?

Why isn't she replying!

Is she angry?

Many things kept going in and out of my mind but nothing really bothered me for long.

However, I was up the entire night staring at my cell phone as if it were the one whom I had asked to marry. My phone screen started appearing a lot prettier after all the staring it got from me that night!

I swear on god, I had never stayed up all night before an exam in the manner I stayed up waiting for an answer from her end!

She had become the heart of my temple of thought and her thoughts were nothing but a storm driven on my skin which gave me the feeling of being human.

Sunrise.

Everything was happening in its usual manner yet everything seemed completely different than what I felt usually.

I was wary to almost everything and even after being a person who worked out regularly; I started getting a feeling of being extremely feeble from within.

Half of the day went by in a jiffy and there was no news from her.

But, as soon as I got over with my lunch break I got a call!

There were only six words that I could hear before there was silence on the other end:

"I want to meet you now!"

My heart started dancing hub-ba-hub-ba once I got to hear her voice.

It was perhaps the best medicine to my wary self.

Nothing mattered to me at that time except for the fact that she had wished to meet me!

We were at two different corners of the city but, could the distance actually be a factor that separated us?

I flung all the work that I had on hand and scampered to the nearest subway.

She had called.

She wanted to meet... ME.

Blood gushed through my veins at a rapid pace. I could literally feel my heart trying to tear through my rib cage and jump out ahead of me...

Sometimes I actually looked down to confirm if it hadn't popped out while beating at that rapid speed!

My face had turned red with all the running that I had to do.

I somehow managed my hair and tried putting on the most decent look that I could at that moment before I actually made an appearance in front of her.

But, all of that didn't actually make a difference at that time!

When I finally reached, panting, sweating and out of breath, I asked-

"Hi! *(trying to catch my breath):* So, why did you call me?"

"Well.... you're the one who started all of this. You tell me."

Now all the so called dreams that I had during the previous night came as a flash.

Though as a vision, I understood what I was actually thinking of at that time.

There were loads that I had to express which I had thought of o'er the night!

I recapitulated every bit of those thoughts and told her -

"Please don't get me wrong.

The other day when you were talking about your getting married I felt really possessive about you and couldn't think of losing you.

Nothing came to my mind... Nothing but the fact that, I like you so much...!

...So much that, even the very thought of losing you was unbearable.

Whatever came to my mind has been spoken and no matter what happens I don't want this to hamper our friendship in any manner.

You are my best friend and will always be.

I am receptive to whatever you say but, please don't let any of this come between our friendship.

I might be okay in losing you as a lover but, I can never afford to lose a friend like you.

You are free to take your decisions and I don't want to influence them in any manner.

Take as much time as you want to but please do think over the whole thing with a cool mind.

You don't have to rush to any decision. Okay?"

She remained quiet and blinked her eyes and I got my answer.

There was this beautiful smile on her face that brought peace to my heart.

Everything about her was so beautiful at that moment that, I felt like giving her a kiss on her forehead and hugging her.

But I didn't...

There was more that I wished to express but, I didn't know what else I could've spoken of at that moment!

Karan-"You didn't have to!

That was a really understanding and mature thing that you had spoken of!

I'm happy to hear it!"

Adarsh-"What happened after that?"

"All that she had to say had been expressed with that blink of her eyes.

Nothing else was needed to be mentioned!

There was a brief moment of silence between us after which she told me that it was time she returned home as the duration for which she had taken permission from her mother was about to get over.

I decided not to force her to stay.

We walked in opposite directions bidding adieu to each other.

But as I walked away on my path, I took out my cell phone and texted her-

"...And listen- What I just can't say in front of you is that I LOVE YOU""

Abhay (adjusting the pillow in his lap): "What the F*** man!

All of this actually happened with my bro and I didn't get to know any of it.

Very sad!"

Karan: "Now would seriously not be a good time to pause Rohit...

What happened next?

I wanna know the entire thing!"

Rohit was thirsty.

His legs had gone off to sleep while he had been narrating the entire story; so; he rose from his position and walked to the refrigerator to fetch him a bottle of water.

While all of this was going on no one spoke a word in the room.

There was a pin drop silence in the room and everybody simply stared at Rohit.

Rohit reclaimed his position and after a deep sigh continued:

"Where was I? Oh yes...I texted her.

Well... After that I got a text from her."

Then without saying any further he took his cell phone from Adarsh and started searching for something.

After a while when he was done with his searching he showed a message, which read:

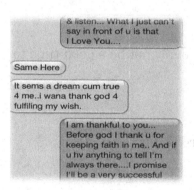

Karan: "One thing's for sure that you are not making this up. At least show us the name buddy..."

Rohit: "...Forget it.

I said no names and I mean it. So please..."

Adarsh: "...You know how he is! Once he has made up his mind he doesn't give a damn to what others say. So let it be!"

Rohit (*smiling*): "My hands were cold and my head was boiling hot.

My heart was on a gala spree!

Words will always be insufficient to describe how I felt at that moment. *(Specifically point to Adarsh)*- ...and that's when I had got into a relationship brother!"

Adarsh: "Great Man! Why didn't you let us know about this at that time?"

"Ah...Bunk it! All this is history, now."

Abhay, Karan and Adarsh *(together)*: "What??"

"Yeah...we did date for some time and eventually there were certain issues due to which we had to separate."

Adarsh-"What issues?"

"The regular; family ones... her upbringing couldn't allow herself to be with me.

There was always a concern and fear once she had accepted the fact that she had started loving me.

Somewhere, between all this I realized that I was losing the person that I had fallen in love with and I couldn't allow myself to do that!

She wasn't the same anymore and coz of all this; even I started falling weak.

There were moments when she would break down stating she could never imagine herself standing up straight; in front of her father; debating on such issues.

I did try and support her as much as I could but...

I guess we were more liberal being friends...

Dating simply wasn't our cup of tea."

Karan: "So you guys broke up?"

Rohit: "Yeah...We did.

It was a mutual decision and perhaps for the better of our career prospects as well.

Her heart was content that she didn't have to speak on such issues in front of her parents and me... I found my friend with whom I had fallen in love!"

Karan-"...Crap! At least you could've given it another shot!"

"I would've done anything and everything to the greatest extent possible.

But, letting her go was the first and the only thing that my best friend had asked of me ... I couldn't deny her!

These decisions can't be imposed.

If that was what she wanted; I think I justified my act by not pursuing any further.

Yes…I did have to keep a stone on my heart when I had to take this decision, but- hey; anything for her!

Abhay: "Come on man! If she was so much to you then why did you give up on her so easily?

I agree sacrificing personal lives for the sake of elders is nothing but an invention of the bourgeoisie!

People do that at a mass, but, I always considered you to be different.

I always thought you would set an example for everybody by leading a life in which you would be able to draw a line between respect; and falling to conservatism.

But now you have proven that; it's always easier said than done!

Blabber mouth!"

Rohit: "The day I admit that human life can be ruled by a reason, I'll be destroying all the possibilities that I'll have in my life.

I have the same opinion to that of yours' brother and I assure you, that I will not be acting like those diachronic dullards who are ready to exterminate their souls for the sake of following some anserine societal norm.

Nevertheless, what happened between the two of us is quite complicated for me to explain as of now.

It is a perplexed situation that cannot be decrypted in words; given my current situation.

Let the entire episode remain between the two of us.

She and I are best friends and shall always be.

Yes, I still love her but, you're wrong if you think that the joy of life comes principally from human relationships.

Some things take some time before you can actually understand them.

...Such was our friendship.

Who said that a boy and a girl can't be best friends?

To hang out with each other, you don't always have to be in a relationship!

I agree that there are a number of people on this planet; who term two best friends of the opposite sexes as lovers whenever they are found alone in each other's company.

But, I don't care what people say...

I can't live a lie by not accepting the fact that she is my best friend and I can't allow any kind of social barrier to come between our relations.

There may be a million social blockades between us but, she is an educated girl and she will understand how a line can be drawn to end the baseless communal customs that are still being advocated, yet...

...Honestly speaking, I've grown as an individual and that's only because of her. She has made me into a more responsible and a more understanding person than what I could've ever been.

I am really happy for her!!"

Adarsh: "What's the current scene?

If all of it ended so well then why are you so upset?"

Rohit *(smiling in despair):* "Remember me telling you about the unbearable idea of not having to get to see her more often once she got married?"

If raindrops tasted like honeydew
And my wishes for you came true
I would sing songs to the open sea
The setting sun as a backdrop and
nothing between you and me

As mountains store a solemn play
Depicting a thoughtful wonder-bay
Watching dahlias twining a merry lee
Setting my heart to a joyous spree

Matter not days when the sun forgets to shine
Coz my heart which loves you
shall keep saying you're mine
Silent winds crossing borders ashore
Will kiss your lips as I shall keep
on loving you evermore

Perhaps the waters might forget they've to flow
But that won't stop my love to grow
Chirping birds singing across the nations
Will portray my love through their emotions

And if that's not all that you want to hear
I'll hope for the heavens to persevere
To bridge the spaces that separates all time
For me to shew my love is divine

So, what if you fear your heart'll stop to beat
I'm pretty sure it's done a feat
that it can never repeat
As my heart is nothing but all yours
And if one stops you shall always have
mine that will forever be yours

Chapter 2

Annihilated Aspirations

"The great drama of life, with its likes and dislikes, its loves and hates, its ambitions and strivings, and manifold ideas, inspirations, aspirations, is absolutely foreign to space, and could never in any way be discovered in space.

So human history has its seat in the invisible...!"

-The Religion of the Samurai

S aying this, he flung his phone on the bed and moved towards the balcony.

Abhay and Karan checked his cell phone and realized that all the evidences that he had shown till now were nothing but a hoax!

All the message conversations were photo shopped.

None of it was true.

Karan- "Why, the heck, did you fool around with us?

If you hadn't wished to tell us the truth in the first place; you could've resisted yourself from narrating a lie...

But this... This is preposterous!!!"

Rohit lay preserved in his vignettes. With a wry smile on his face he moved a bit around the room; and then; as if he were to give a speech; turned towards his audience with; perhaps the most defining expression he could put on and continued...

"You guys are well aware of the fact that I fancy calling myself- 'Magicman'.

The very reason I tend to do so is because I'm filled with high spirits and I always find ways to lift myself up when low.

Whenever someone is feeling low, I am the one who takes the initiative to cheer him or her.

This is the way I have lived and I will continue to express myself wherever and whenever it'll be necessary. But now, I ask you-

What would you do if all your emotions and spirit have drained out?

What would you do if you were dead from the inside and there were absolutely no emotions left in your heart?"

Adarsh- "Buddy, we have always been there to support you! But, we can never be of any help unless you share your problems with us. I'm pretty damn sure we will find a solution to it."

Rohit-"Dude, It's true that I've loved someone with all my heart. She has become an indispensable part of my life but..."

Abhay *(jumping as if he had found a solution to everything)*-"Ultimately she's not with you anymore! That's the reason for everything."

Karan- "Stop doing that, will you?

Let Rohit speak before arriving to your unwarranted conclusions."

There was silence in the room once again.

No one spoke; however, there were a few minor adjustments in the way everyone sat.

Rohit *(taking a big sigh)* - "Whatever I've told you so far is true. In fact, even the part about our break up is true. We did break up once. Initially, she was very scared to step out of what she termed as her culture.

She always feared of what her parents might have to say and what society would comment on getting to know that she had been liberal enough to choose her own life companion.

She kept reminding me that her father held a very respectful position in the society and that; her act of deciding who her life partner would be; would hemorrhage that severely.

I tried being supportive on every instance but time and again she would fall apart and break into tears exclaiming that she would never be able to tell about her likings to her parents.

The only way; according to her; was that both of us forgot each other and let things be the way they were...

Romance, as per her version, looks good only in the cinemas!! It screws all life forms in practicality!

I didn't prefer to push her on this issue.

All I knew was that I loved her, and literature seemed life.

What she termed as conceptual paradoxes was something I strived for in reality!

I couldn't imagine letting her go and no matter how bad she felt of her situation; I would keep on explaining to her that the reward to this entire struggle was being together for a lifetime.

This was indeed a very hefty proposal.

To accompany it, there were a lot of promises as well. And after all that was done; she would finally place her confidence in me and happiness would be back on our faces.

But, these moments were nothing different from passing clouds which would waver from time to time.

Nevertheless, somewhere deep within my heart, I had a belief... a belief that she would be mine for a lifetime.

And this was the only thing that gave me strength; no matter how trying were the circumstances!"

Curiosity along with confusion filled the room.

Everybody wanted to know who the mystery girl in Rohit's life actually was.

Seriousness had finally beseeched its companion-humor; to give it way to the center stage!

The powwows and oh-how were soon replaced with mum mouths and everybody kept gazing at the story-teller who kept going on!

Amidst all these, Rohit never raised his head while he spoke.

He simply kept looking at the ground as he continued...

"I needn't go on and explain what kind of a person I am.

I have been, and am, friends with quite a number of girls but, when it came to choosing a person with whom I would have liked to spend the rest of my life with; I wandered in search of my other half.

Searching for my soul companion... The one who would grab hold of my life while taking hold of my heart!

The one who would complete me and make me believe in love stories all over again!

Yes, I do pretend a lot. But, beneath this pretentious self-there's a lad who is absolutely clean at psyche and expects her to be the same.

Money… looks…everything else is secondary. The only criterion that I wanted to be complied with was the connection of hearts…

…And with her…. Well… our hearts blended into one!"

Saying this Rohit walked away from his position towards the refrigerator and gulped down a bottle of water.

He then put his hands in his denims pockets and seemed clueless as to how he would continue narrating.

The continuous jingling of the keys kept in his pocket along with a few coins irritated his fellow inmates but, no one actually complained.

A little bit of irritation was manageable when compared to the tales from Rohit's life; that were being unveiled.

A few pitches and glitches occurred; after which everyone adjusted into his own miasma!

Adarsh- "Twenty years….Twenty years is the age of our friendship and what it has taught me is that standing up and being there is what counts in friendship; o'er the time spent together.

Your ins and outs are well known mates to my awareness and explanations to your persona aren't required brother.

So you chose an ideal life partner... I won't really want to know her name but again, there's no forcing.

...Do that only when you deem it to be correct.

But, what I would request you; is to go on and tell me what is that bothers my brother so much that I am losing the Magicman I knew!

Please Rohit, set yourself free... speak out!"

Rohit tried matching words to his emotions and even though he stammered a lot in trying to do so; he somehow managed to fit them in his figure of speech:

"I...I had made her a set of promises.

At every instance, where I had made her feel strong of our relationship, I also promised her that no matter what happened; the magic for which the Magicman was known; would always shield her; under all circumstances!

Yes; we were enthusiastic! And many a time common-sense did try to sway away in enthusiasm.

So, out of the many promises that I had made; I promised her that no matter what happened I would never let any of our emotions over-ride the practicality of the situation!

Love often paralyzes the rationality of one's mind and so; I promised to be defunct to its nausea!

But, I broke that promise...

Abhay-"Don't tell me you..."

"Ah! Grow up Abhay! It's nothing of that sort! Not even close to what you think!"

"...then?"

"Well; all she wanted was that either I or any of my family members would approach her father to express my willingness to marry her!

I was in complete agreement to this and therefore promised her that no matter what happens, she would never have to do the talking regarding any of this!

But as the situations kept changing; I realized that it would be better if she started with the initial talking!

It wasn't that I was running away from my promises..."

Karan-"But, wasn't that something which she had clearly accepted to be out of her capacity! I mean; weren't those the basic issues which she had highlighted upfront?"

"Yes; they were...

And for this very reason, I requested her that if she was incapable of talking to her father she should approach him either by way of her sister or her mother!

Girls find that way easier and if the wife is taken care of- half of the problem is mostly done away with!"

Adarsh-"You're such an imp! Make the promised and then break them... you shrewd flim-flam!"

"Hey... I did discuss the entire issue with my dad and only after having done so I felt that no parent to a girl would feel pleasant on coming to know of her daughter's affair from somebody else other than her daughter!

My dad told me that he had no issues to approach her father, but...

Abhay *(exclaiming in astonishment)* - "Hang on... Uncle knows about all this?"

Rohit *(nodding his head in affirmation)* - "...She was gutted that I was not sticking to the initial promises!"

Karan-"... Why wouldn't she?"

"To be honest, I myself didn't like the fact that I was straying from my word.

But, I had done it only coz I thought that it would have been more sensible that I did so!

I assured her that whatever was being done was to ameliorate her place in our relationship.

All I requested her was to have faith in me; and that she had in plenty."

Adarsh- "So what happened when she spoke of you to her parents?

Did they disapprove you?

Is this why you are behaving all lost?"

Rohit *(raising his hands)* - "Everything aren't bread and butter!"

Adarsh- Then what is it... lasagna?"

"Dude....."

"Sorry... please continue!"

"Grazie! I'm honored!

She needed to know how she should go about all this so that she could communicate about our relationship to her parents!

Thus, we decided to meet before she did all the talking!

Meeting wasn't an issue at that time as she was over with her exams and had recommenced her internship!

The office hood cafeteria welcomed a paradise but that wasn't for long....

Work pressure was increasing after I had got my firm converted into a limited company.

I had to do a lot of travelling as this was one of the basic requirements of our business expansion.

Even on the day, when we had decided to have a talk on this issue, I was literally in a different city!

The day... It keeps flashing in my mind all the time!"

Rohit remained silent for some time. He shook his wrist watch; then browsed through something in his cell phone and sighed before he continued:

I had left work post-lunch giving a medical excuse and once out; I drove to pick her up from her work place!"

Karan *(putting up a smile on his face)* - "Typical you!"

Rohit paused for a moment and gave an ironic smile.

Nevertheless, the seriousness that had gathered on his face all this time, while he was narrating never disappeared.

He gasped a huge breath and suggested Karan to allow him to complete the story without being interrupted any further.

Adarsh, Karan and Abhay exchanged eye contacts and there were slight smiles on their faces.

But, no one dared to speak a word.

All of them remained quiet and the setting was ready.

"It didn't take me much time to pick her up.

The roads; at that time of the day were void of any traffic and it hardly took me any time which otherwise would've taken hours...

As soon as I picked her up; we drove as far as possible so that we could escape to a place away from the city, where it would be only the two of us!

Throughout the journey, she had grabbed hold of my hand tightly; which was engaged in changing the gears.

We hardly had any verbal communication!

As a matter of fact, we never had to...

The presence of her touch was working more than what the exchange of words could've ever done."

Abhay- "Aww! That's so romantic."

"Dude... Could you please shut up?"

"What!!! I was trying to spice things up a bit!"

".... Just shut up!"

Abhay started smiling but stopped on what he was going to say.

Seeing him smile, even Adarsh and Karan found a reason to grin.

However, there was no tittle-tattle to interrupt Rohit as he spoke...

"I drove for an hour or so after which we reached a 'Dhaba'... the one that is on the South National Highway.

Given the fact that it was a weekday and the time when we had reached there, the setting there was perfect for the two of us to converse in solitude.

I had purposely placed an order for such items which would take a lot of preparation time so that I could have an excuse of being alone with her for some more time.

Moreover, hadn't the steward taken our order he would hover around us!

Karan-"You're rambunctious!"

Rohit-"huh...!"

Karan-"Yeah...!"

Adarsh-"Don't think over it! He keeps blabbering for no reason!

…What did you talk to her?"

"Initially we were sitting on opposite sides of the table. But, as soon as the steward left the room, I swapped sides to sit next to her.

Then, she grabbed me tightly by my arm and told:

"Rohit, promise me you will never leave me. Promise me that you are mine!"

I didn't understand the reason for her sudden emotional outburst.

She was quite normal all this while, but from her reaction it seemed as if she had been waiting for the right moment to express herself!

The moment she did so, I felt as if I were holding the most fragile piece of God's creation in my arms.

Clueless as to what to do, I hugged her and promised that I would never let her go; no matter what happened!

No matter how trying the situations became; the Magicman would always be by her side; at all costs!

She didn't utter a word but her grip on my arm became tighter.

I then kissed her on her forehead and…"

Abhay-"Ooooooo!!!!"

All of it was nothing but entertainment to Abhay who kept finding reasons to giggle on Rohit's narratives!

Rohit on the other hand turned red and replied in fury:

"Abhay grow up!

You're nothing but a big pervert.

I hate to say this but, yes you are!

You have no idea how special our love is.

Could you please stop comparing love to sex?

Our love is something much pure.

This is the love of my life I'm talking about.

The one with whom I intend to spend my life.

The one whom I intend to bring home-to my parents-to my family!

The one with whom I intend to grow old!

The one who gives me a reason to live!

Dude…seriously!"

All of a sudden the smile from Abhay's face seemed to have disappeared.

He straightened his back and sat still, but now, with a much more serious look on his face.

Abhay-"Okay I'm sorry. This won't happen again. Trust me."

Rohit- "It better not!"

Adarsh-"Ssshh! Stop it! Both of you!

…Rohit, he's an ass****. Don't take him too seriously. And if possible, try bunking the descriptivism else he'll continue being satirical!

What happened next?"

Rohit-"I told P…

(He was about to complete his sentence. But, as he was about to do so he realized that he had made a set of statements that forbade him to speak of certain things he had desired to do!

Therefore, changing the way he had intended to continue!)

… I told precisely what I had to speak.

I reminded her that her parents were and would always be her first priority!

Nothing could overrule their decision!

However, she should definitely give in her best efforts to make her parents aware as to how she felt for me!"

Rohit paused...

His eyes filled up as he tried recalling what had happened after that!

But, somehow he prevented them from coming out and gave way to a fake laugh...

"Why are things always so tough?

I love her bro...

I love her like anything!

Isn't that all that's needed?

Why are there so many hindrances and tests when the only fault that I had committed was falling in love with my best friend...?

It wasn't as if I were the only one who felt so!

The feeling was mutual!

And... this was not at all infatuation! We thought over it a number of times! ...And every time I questioned my feelings for her, my heart would keep telling me-'she's the one!'

Why...?"

This time the tears couldn't stop.

They trickled down his cheeks and told an untold story which he wasn't strong enough to elaborate at that time.

Adarsh- "Rohit... calm down!

We will always be there for you whenever you seek any help!

Just tell us what needs to be done.

Anything for you... All I'll ask of is the time and venue and... Boom- I'll be there.

Cheer up Brother! Crying ain't a solution! You're a strong lad!

... And Piyush gets married in a few hours from now! We can't allow him to see you shattered just before his marriage... can we?

Once we reach home; we'll find a solution to everything!

Till then; try being strong!

And if there's anything that you want to share; feel free!

It will help you relieve the emotional pressure that is bothering you..."

Rohit hugged Adarsh.

This was perhaps the best reply he could've given at that time.

...Or perhaps, something that he most needed!

Rohit *(Gathering himself)*-"Her parents are very conservative!

Considering the modern world we live in, I found it really hard to believe how conservative people can actually be!

People are indifferent to each other. They have the same two hands and two legs and one face that everyone has... But it's what's inside these bodies that differentiate one from the other. And strangely; in many cases these insides haven't evolved brother! They have simply learnt the art of hiding!

Somewhere I also feel that conservatism is important as the roots of our ethnicity are somewhere linked to our being conservative.

The basic ideology behind conservatism is leaving things the way they are. But one has to acknowledge the fact that the things that are left alone are actually left to the torrents of change.

The basic ingredients to conservatism involve people who are absolutely unwilling to accept a change in the way they think; the parous of what the people might say and the fear of becoming an outlaw to the established vogue...

There is a very thin line between the conservation of culture and conservatism and people often ameliorate the former to the latter per se their comfort!

Change is a companion to the youth and a child to the existing culture!

What change lacks is experience and on this very ground; most of the battles are lost!

But one has to acknowledge the fact that if changes come in the way we live, then reforms have to be bought to the outlook of the thinking mind; lest they are inculcated at a steady pace!

Change is inevitable... Sooner or later, it will definitely happen!

The greater the delay, the more will we be welcoming an emotional outburst...

I tried to make her understand in a number of ways that even though she was scared of going and talking to her father; it was something which she would eventually have to accept in front of him.

Directly or indirectly, she would have to face the situation. Succumbing to her fear wasn't a feasible solution.

She felt she was more open to her mother than to her father and therefore decided to have a talk with her first.

… But, even this was something that scared the bejeezus out of her!

But, after all the emotional speeches that I had made and after a lot of convincing, she finally gathered enough courage to go and have a talk with her mother."

Adarsh-"You let her approach her mother directly?

Wasn't it a better plan to take any one of her sisters in confidence before she did that?"

"One of her sisters, Sweta; knew about the two of us for a very long time.

We had her support on whatever step we took next!

She was well aware as to where I was working and who I was in person!

And taking everything into consideration, even she had approved the idea of having a talk with her mother as an indirect yet better way of approaching her father!"

Adarsh-"Okay"

"Her other siblings weren't aware of the Magicman affair!

So we had to keep the matters only between the three of us.

However this wasn't the subject matter of botheration as Sweta was the second eldest amongst the siblings and she was quite a responsible girl and one who was well aware of the likes and dislikes of everyone in her family!

Adarsh-"Nice...! So everything was well planned!

Darn you Rohit... You found me of no worth!

Else you would've definitely discussed this matter with me!

... And who knows if things had clicked between me and Sweta!

Hahaha!

But seriously ... On a more serious note, I thought we always had this bond, yet you proved it to be false today!

Times have changed and so have you!

Today, I have realized the fact that having a girl in your life has severely affected our friendship!"

"...Not at all! You have been and will always be more than a brother to me!

It's just that things were moving so quickly that I hardly got any time to think!

You know how it is in a girl's family; as soon she turns old enough to get married!

Something or the other kept going on at her home and a step had to be taken at our end...

...The sooner the better!"

Adarsh-"Hmm...! It's okay! ...I understand! Bunk it...Hokum dekko!"

"Dude...!"

"Don't dude me... I got my answer... just tell me what happened after that!"

"We started by laying the foundation!

Be it big or small, she along with Sweta sought all opportunities to sing songs of praises for me as a friend!

The basic idea behind this was to make her mother like me."

Abhay- "Ooo... Can I have the privilege of knowing what's so praiseworthy about you?"

"Abhay... I seriously feel like punching you in the face!"

Karan-"You gave her ideas to your extolment?

That is weird! A bit too weird...!"

"Actually I never had to! She knew me more than I knew myself!

On certain instances, I wasn't even aware that I had developed certain habits which; on the other hand were well known to her!

Her mother had started getting hints but she never really reacted to her daughter's sudden growing interests in me.

Initially, she took me as an influential friend; whom her daughter couldn't stop talking to.

This went on for some time after which she decided that it was time to reveal what I actually meant to her daughter!

Sweta was present in the room when she had dared to do this!

Even though she had to do all the talking on her own, the presence of her sister in the room gave her immense moral support!

... and after a lot of hesitation when she finally spoke what she was supposed to speak of; her mother turned savage to know that her daughter had dared to have a free heart.

She completely denied the idea of her daughter falling in love with some guy and her expressing the willingness to marry him...

Good girls shouldn't fall in love before marriage! This was her perception...

... And this was not the only instance when her mother had been persuaded.

In fact, she had requested her mother to hear her heart out a number of times; sometimes, as an earnest plea or sometimes imploring to spare a thought for me!

The only outcome of this persuasion was that she was warned never to even dare to take up such an issue in front of her father..."

Karan-"Fish..."

"I sought that it was better that I hadn't come in the picture at that moment!

Coz, if any step would've been taken from my end, her father could've been hurt even more; considering the description of his mentation that I had perceived from the narratives given by his daughters.

An initial denial was always there on the cards. It was almost obvious considering the magnitude to which she solicited all faults to her feminism!

Even though she hadn't accepted it; I, on the other hand, was well in anticipation of it.

There was an emotional outburst each and every time when she was denied permission and to this I would have to keep on convincing her to pursue her happiness.

I would give her strength by letting her know that eventually everything would be fine.

I would keep telling her that perhaps sub-consciously her mother had not accepted the fact that her daughter could take such an important decision of her life on her own.

She was, perhaps for this reason, being a bit protective.

An initial pooh-pooh would have always been there; on the coattails but, she would have to remain strong to prevent the faltering of her trust.

But, my soul strengthening speeches were nothing when compared to a simple stare from her mother.

Every time it happened, it would be more than enough; to scare her down to her roots...

I begged her to try and convince her mother one last time before an alternative could be thought of.

And when she did so, the response remained the same...

She buzzed me and wept bitterly:

"Rohit forget me...

Nothing can happen of us.

My parents will never accept you!

I simply can't go in front of them and speak my heart out!

You have to figure out a way of living without me!

You have to figure out a life of which I am not a part!

You have to let me go Rohit...

Please forgive me."

Saying this she disconnected the call.

I tried calling her up a number of times but she kept disconnecting my calls!

I was really worried and wanted to talk to her.

Though, I wasn't aware of the subject matter of our conversation but, I just wanted to hear her voice and make her realize that no matter what happened I would have always been with her.

I texted her hoping that she would communicate via texts in case she wasn't relenting to talk o'er the phone!

I wanted to make her realize that though her mother had not agreed on us, she still stood a chance if she had a talk directly with her father!"

Adarsh-"...And the cat went inside the tiger's den?

Rohit...How could you so easily ask her to do something of that sort?"

"Yes; that was indeed something that she feared the most.

But, she....!"

Karan- "Did she...?"

"I would like to thank Sweta for this!

At times, she is very childish!

I was anticipating her next move to be to go and have a conversation directly with her father!

But, thanks to Sweta; coz at that time her infantilism made things very easy!"

Adarsh-"Okies... A wife's sister is always half the homemaker!

Hence proved!

...so what did she do?"

"She has this habit of running around here and there.

She loves dancing and one day while she was dancing she conveyed the message of her sister's affair to her father!"

Adarsh and Karan *(simultaneously)*-"What...?"

"I know... I reacted in the same way when I came to know about it!"

Karan-"Obviously... coz that's not infantilism!

That's stupidity?"

"Her father interpreted the message conveyed by her sister almost instantaneously!

The very next question that he asked was-'Whatever Sweta tried to enact- is it true?'

To this, all she could do was keep staring at his feet!

She never replied!"

Abhay-"Did her father hit her?"

Well... He did slap her... But not literally... His stare was enough!

He was livid that his eldest daughter had lost all courage to make an eye contact!

Her father fumed in anger and left the room immediately!

He avoided talking at home for the next couple of days, and his reactions on the entire episode were very limited.

I couldn't understand how her parents were pretending to be oblivious to their daughter's feeling.

These were really perplexing moments for the both of us.

But, somewhere deep within; his mind remained occupied.

He had been thinking a lot o'er it and I had seriously no idea as to what it was!

On my part; I simply prayed for things to be normal and in my favor!

A few a days later, he told his family o'er dinner that he was willing to have a look at the personal bio-data of the guy who was continuously being praised by his two daughters..."

Abhay-"Wow! You must've been sky high at that moment!"

"Indeed I was! And as soon as I came to know about this, I wasted no time in mailing her my bio-data!"

Karan *(interrupting)*-"What on earth did you write in your bio-data?

...If someone had told me to do the same I would've kept staring into emptiness before I actually wrote something."

Rohit- "Even I had no idea as to what I had to include in it while I was drafting it. I simply kept writing everything which I thought would impress her father.

Big or small issues- I incorporated almost all matters and mailed it to her immediately so that she could show it to her father.

I even had a talk with Sweta regarding this so that I could have a neutral opinion on what her father adored and abhorred.

...When she presented my resume to her father; she also mentioned the fact that my dad knew everything about us and that he was also willing to have a talk with him if he found it comfortable enough to do so!

Her dad remained quiet for a very long time and didn't utter a single word and she simply kept staring at his feet.

He was already very angry with his daughter daring to fall in love and...

Her dad read her and then sighed.

'I'll do what's best for you...!'

Adarsh-"I feel so left out buddy... Sigh!"

So did they match your horoscope and shit...?

I mean... the bio data...

After she gave it to her father, did he calculate all that crap to reject you on that ground?"

"I... I... I really don't know how I can describe what happened next.

I mean, our anxiety was at its peak when she submitted my profile in front of her father!

Tears filled up his eyes once again as he tried to find the correct words which would describe the state the affairs!

There was a small pause before he exclaimed in disbelief:

"Never did her father consider me!

He didn't even have a look at my resume nor the pictures that I had mailed!

As a matter of fact, the mere idea of his daughter telling him of a boy whom she liked was something he just couldn't cope with.

For this very reason; he prohibited her from going to work from that very moment and confiscated her cell phone!

I had had been trying to get in touch with her ever since that incident but I just can't get connected to her.

I tried calling her up, texting her, mailing her but, nothing ... nothing worked.

I am very worried for her.

Extremely worried!

Later, after a few days, while her father was at work and her mom was taking a shower she got a chance to use her cell phone.

She was weeping.

She cried and told me:

"Rohit, I can sacrifice myself to my father's decision but I simply can't disobey him.

I owe him lots which I perhaps can never pay back.

I assure you that you are the only one whom I have ever loved in this life and if I am married to someone else, then, only my body will be his.

My soul is yours and only yours..."

Saying this she disconnected the call and I haven't heard from her ever since then.

All roads to her now seem to have been closed...

(Tears started rolling down Rohit's cheeks.)

I am devastated from within Adarsh...Completely destructed!

All I ever did was to love her to the greatest extent I possibly could; but, I fail to find a reason as to where I went wrong!

Why didn't her father consider me?

Was it a bit too much to ask for?

Can't a girl form an opinion on her likes and dislikes?

Am I that bad a person that her father wouldn't even consider giving me a chance?"

Adarsh- "Dude, calm down.

Whining won't help you figure out a way!

I bet some alternative solutions can still be opted for!

If everything would've been easy to get then it's true worth would always be undermined!

If you are made to suffer to get the love of your life then you will always understand its value and will treasure it forever."

"Bro, I don't understand a shit of what you're saying.

All I know is that I love her and I want her in my life!

The philosophies with which you are filling my ears are nothing but Greek to me!

I don't know what to say!

But, what I do know is that I need her!"

Abhay- "Don't worry bro!

Let time play its role. True love always comes back...

These issues are simply putting your love to the test!

And believe me; if the two of you are really meant for each other then, nothing can come between you two!

You just need to hang in there!

Everything will be fine!

Trust me!"

Rohit-"...While I was online on Facebook a few days back; Sweta started chatting with me.

She told me that her sister hadn't been keeping well.

She had stopped eating and wasn't able to sleep properly for the past one week.

And to be true to you, that's the same scenario with me even now.

Sweta told me that her father sought her sister's marriage to be the best cure to her ill behavior.

So, their parents decided to accept the marriage proposal from Bangalore!

They haven't confirmed the marriage proposal as of now but, they have conveyed the broker to schedule a meeting at the earliest.

After having heard this, I tried requesting my father if he could do something regarding this...

And he did try!

He did express his willingness to go and have a talk with her father regarding this issue but...

My dad went on to say that since I was the groom, ethnically it should be her father who should take the initiating step!

However, he didn't pay any attention to this tradition as it was I- his son, whose happiness was all that he endeavored!

But after her father had blocked off all modes of communication to himself; my father couldn't really . understand how he could persuade him!

He wanted his cerebration to be communicated but at the same time he did not want to seem too trying!

There was an extent to which he could try after which he told me that if her father didn't deem me to be worth considering; then there was nothing else that could be done at his end!

She was his daughter and it was his life after all!

I have no idea as to what I can do to bring her back into my life!

But...I can't live without her.

I can't imagine her being in somebody else's arms.

I can't bro...I simply can't."

Saying this he rose from his position.

He was restless and started banging his fists against the wall.

Adarsh, Karan and Abhay had no idea how to react to Rohit's vagary.

All of them stood still.

...Then, in a moment of madness, Rohit rushed out to the balcony and jumped.

Adarsh, Karan and Abhay *(All of them shouting together)* - "Rohit!!!!"

Silence filled the room.

No one spoke.

No one moved.

And Rohit never responded to his friend's call...

Happy Holidays!

My friend moves to a new and better place
And I can't stop him but let go
His place remains empty in my life
Yet I can't do anything but let go
It's like those rivers that keep flowing on
The roads that shall keep going on...

Change is an inevitable thing
Lest you stop to feel your beating heart
Sometime from now we shall all be gone
To different places distant afar
I'll miss your face
Miss your company
But that's something I'll have to bear
As the rivers keep flowing on
And the roads shall keep going on.

We sat and laughed
And shared each other's company
Those days are gone
Now we're both alone
You walk your path
And I walk my own
Yet we cannot stop
And we can't return
Coz the rivers will keep flowing on
And the roads shall keep going on

It's late at night
I'm in solitude
Miss those talks
I had with you

And you have gone
To a better place
And I cannot but let you go
To where you go
As the rivers they keep flowing
And the roads shall keep going on
They teach us so that life's this
Where we have no choice but, move on...

Chapter 3

Requiem for a Dream

A vast expanse of trees and grasslands neared Rohit with the passage of each second.

Odd, that such a magnificent hotel had been constructed amidst this greenery.

Rohit knew that he had left his friends with a lot of unanswered questions.

He knew that all Abhay, Karan and Adarsh had wanted to do was to help him, but, he had left all of them helpless.

The November breeze which travelled from the west, in its weary way, caused the trees to sway and a few leaves floated down to the ground below him. But Rohit could hardly see any of those leaves lying over there.

How great could've things been if everything had worked out!

Now, it was too late for anything to be done.

How hard had life been in the past few weeks!

Each moment... Each second... All flashed memories which he had earned over his lifetime.

Rohit walked over to the parapet; climbed over and sat on it with his legs hanging in the emptiness and his back to the door of the balcony.

He closed his eyes and took in the air.

It was still and fresh. He could hear everything that painted the aura of his surroundings. The cooing of the pigeons; the stridulating of the crickets; all seemed so white, serene and peaceful.

And then Rohit started wondering how long had he been sitting there!

He felt his body going numb with pain. At that moment; the moment of impact; nothing seemed to matter. His family; his friends; his love; his life-everything seemed to be an illusion to divert his mind from reality!

His body gave away and slowly slipped away from the parapet into the emptiness.

As he fell, he felt weightlessness and for the first time in days he started feeling light headed, light hearted.

He opened his eyes just as his body hit the ground and he saw her standing o'er there...

She looked as beautiful as always and she smiled at him.

Rohit reached out his arms towards her but then, everything started becoming dark...

"Impeded wish is also suffering.

We do not wish to be associated with things or persons we detest, nor do we wish to be separated from things or persons we love.

Our cherished desires are not, however, always gratified. What we least expect or what we least desire is often thrust on us.

At times such unexpected unpleasant circumstances become so intolerable and painful that weak ignorant folk are compelled to commit suicide as if such an act would solve the problem.

Real happiness is found within, and is not to be defined in terms of wealth, power, honors or conquests.

If such worldly possessions are forcibly or unjustly obtained, or are misdirected, or even viewed with attachment, they will be a source of pain and sorrow for the possessors."

-Lord Buddha

"ROHIT...!"- *Abhay, Karan and Adarsh were stupefied.*

They stood still without having any clue as to how they should react to the situation.

Then all of a sudden:

Adarsh *(rushing towards the door)* - "Oh-Come one you morons!

I want both of you downstairs immediately!"

Adarsh's words seemed to have woken Abhay and Karan from a trance.

The reaction to his words was almost spontaneous and all of them rushed downstairs...

Abhay-"What the heck...!

What the heck...!

What the heck...!

Somebody please tell me that I'm dreaming.

This can't be true!

This can't be true.

Rohit, my bro..."

Karan- "Abhay please be quiet.

This is not the right time for you to yammer.

Rohit is in need more than ever.

Be brave and let us face what has happened. Stop behaving like this!"

As soon as they reached downstairs, they couldn't believe the vision that they witnessed.

Rohit lay still on the ground as his knackered eyes exchanged a frailing vision with his friends.

He was still trying to smile but somehow didn't find any energy within himself which allowed him to do so.

A drop of tear trickled down his cheek and blended with the blood which had splattered all around him.

His temple had smashed badly against the floor and the resemblance was nothing different to a watermelon as if it were thrown from a great height.

I did everything that I possibly could!

Why did I deserve this Karan?

Why?

You know- there's this thing that I had never shared with you...

She had been raped when she was young!

I knew this and I wanted her in my life even after knowing this because I had loved her for the person she was.

Her history didn't concern me one bit.

She always told me that she respected me a lot and would never want to lose me.

And, all I wanted was her to be in my life and her father...

(Choking in his own blood)

...Am I a bad guy?

...Am I too ugly?

I understand that her parents will always do what's good for her; but, why were things between us to end like this!

Why can't I...

The flickering eyes couldn't stay afloat any longer...

Rohit slowly closed his eyes and a scream could be heard in the voice of Karan who had been holding his friend in his arms.

His tuxedo was more of a haemal gown which seemed to be a permanent resident to a slaughter house.

Stained... He shouted:

"Wake up Rohit!

Wake up!

You should have never told me about all this.

Why Rohit, Why!

How can she mean everything to you Rohit?

Why didn't you think of your parents before doing this…?

And we had always been there for you…

If only you could've waited…

Wake up buddy!

Please… Don't' leave me like this!"

Karan kept slapping Rohit; but he never woke up…

No one else but silence spoke.

The November wind was perhaps the noisiest element in the aura which had acquired a sense of asphyxiation after all that had just happened.

The moment of impact was painted in crimson.

Four friends at a wedding now seemed to be more of three friends attending a funeral.

The balcony gave way to the rear side of the hotel.

Due to this, the hotel security was unaware of the situation that had come up in the hotel backyard.

Adarsh- "We need to take him to a hospital right now!

I am going to the reception to see if I can manage some help.

Karan, please call up uncle and inform him…"

Adarsh ran towards the reception to seek help and Karan took out his cell phone to call Rohit's father.

"…Namaste uncle!

Karan here!

Uncle I don't know how to put this in front of you but…

Uncle Rohit has jumped off the balcony!"

"What!"

"Uncle… I… I … I can't understand a thing!

I really can't understand what the hell is going on!

He was pretty normal a few moments ago but…!

This act of his came completely out of the blue!

I… I never knew…Uncle…

Even though Karan had been able to gather himself before making the call he somehow couldn't control himself when he heard Rohit's father's voice.

He broke down without knowing what to speak next.

Even Rohit's father had no idea regarding what had struck him.

"Calm down, Beta!

How is he now?

Can he talk? *(Almost breaking into tears)* Is he in his senses?

What has happened to him?"

"Uncle I can't understand a thing.

There's blood everywhere.

Rohit is absolutely still.

He is not moving."

"Take control of the situation Karan!

Worrying won't help!

As far as I know there are no hospitals in Bhimtal.

I will try and make arrangements in Nainital.

Everything will be Ok.

Just pray for your friend.

Try communicating with the hotel manager over there and arrange for some conveyance so that you can take him down to Nainital as early as possible.

I will try and reach as soon as I can.

Till then be brave and manage the whole situation."

"Uncle, Adarsh has gone to arrange for the conveyance. Abhay and I are here with Rohit.

We will keep you updated with whatever happens over here.

Please let us know about the doctor.

Don't you worry; I will manage everything over here uncle.

I will not let anything happen to Rohit.

I think I'll inform Piyush's father as well.

He might be able to help us out as he knows quite a number of people over here.

Please try coming as fast as you can."

Karan's hand shook as he tried to disconnect the call.

Abhay, who stood at a fair distance from Karan and Rohit, was scared to come any closer.

He was merely a spectator who simply couldn't believe the turn of events. The blood; the moaning and the silence in the darkness, shuddered his rachis from the very core.

Being a stranger to all of it was what he actually wanted but, given the situation; running away was not the need of the hour!

Yet bravery didn't catch hold of him; forcing him to take the initiating step.

He gazed into the redness of the flooring and all of this wasn't a comic episode anymore!

The night faded away into the darkness as three friends endeavored to save a friend's life...

Happy Holidays!

Am I in reality or just a strange illusion?
A spell cast on this planet- a façade of a delusion
What's the truth behind this botheration?
Unspoken words behind life's annihilation
Is it just a thought – or a crazy
dream of self-realization!

Can it be an error that they don't see me?
Or is just the time that they don't need me
My lips are sealed yet why am I speaking
I ain't crying yet why do I feel my eyes bleeding
Is it just a thought – or a crazy
dream of self-realization!

Is it just me or are the shadows fading faster
Before it's realized the sun is getting darker
The land remains arid even when it's raining
I may be comforted but why does
the heart keep paining
Is it just a thought – or a crazy
dream of self-realization!

The more and more I ponder -my
life drifts before me
A spawn bred amongst sinners where
the world doesn't need me
I strum my chords, yet why ain't I hearing
Is it too much to ask betwixt all this pain bearing
Is it just a thought – or a crazy
dream of self-realization!

Scar my throat as I play my candidation
Hear me connote careen in exhilaration
The games are played yet no one's wining
Everybody is innocent yet everybody's sinning
Is it just a thought – or a crazy
dream of self-realization!

God knows perhaps why I'm in vexation
Or am I the first to realize our conviction
Days go by and no care for Terra Mater
Life's escapade with rapacity the debater
Is it just a thought – or a crazy
dream of self-realization!

Is it just a thought...?

...Or a crazy dream of self-realization?

Reality seemed like a third world as dreams kept sending a surreal shiver of reality down the spine.

Goosebumps were inmates to open eyes who blamed their being soporific as the mother of all evil!

Rohit; the person who dreamt during the day; deep into the darkness peering for long; remained lying on his bed wondering, fearing, doubting, dreaming...

...Dreaming of dreams no mortal belonging to his schlep had ever dared to dream of!

And when he did realize that he had hit reality four days had gone by!

...Four days since the eyes of the daydreamer met sunlight and all he could woolgather was a blame which punished him to see the dawn before the rest of the world had opened their eyes...

Adarsh, Abhay and Karan who had come to ask for the wellness of their macabre friend; were present in the room!

His parents had never left his side as he tried regaining good health!

And when the frailing eyes did gain consciousness; Rohit found himself to be surrounded by his friends and family!

Everybody waiting for him to wake up!

Praying for him to wake up!

Pleading for him to wake up!

...All this while his soliloquy had raised several questions in the minds of everyone around him!

His body was in pain which was accompanied by a soul that had been awake and had a lot of questions that needed to be asked and answered!

Everybody sighed in relief when they saw Rohit open his eyes...

Delusions were an uncomforting iffy who weren't welcome to the sane minded!

The oppugns, however; which had occupied their minds; were plenty in number and no one was willing to wait; considering the participation they had had in his fantasia!

Nevertheless, the wait wasn't a long one either!

Rohit's eyes audited the entire room in the fraction of a second as it eventually rested on his mother who held his hand as she sat next to him.

"Ma....!"

"Hmmmm..."

His mother didn't utter a word...

Her vision gloomed as tears filled her eyes!

Her grasp on Rohit's hand tightened and apart from this, there wasn't anything else that she did.

Rohit's father- "I feel like giving you one tight slap.

How could you even dream of such a thing?

Rohit-whose nimbus had been tinctured by his mother's touch suddenly, realized that the exhibition of the grey clouds over him wasn't actually over.

There was more to come... More!

...Plenty more!

His dad stared at him like an avenger; questing the reason to his son's thought!

Is Pragya the whole world to you?

Do your mother and I mean nothing?

Look at your mom!

She has been crying ever since you were diagnosed of dengue and admitted in the ICCU!

We haven't had a second's sleep since then!

And while all of us are trying to take care of you; you start murmuring a tale that's way beyond our acceptance!

Rohit!

Is our understanding that weak; that, you were actually considering committing suicide after I had taken the decision of not to persuade Pragya's father any further?

Why Rohit?

Why such a weak sub-conscious mind?

All this time; while you were sedated all of us were appalled at your soliloquize!

I always treated you as a friend and after all that, this is how you think!

I am sad... ashamed... appalled... heart-broken...

Both, your mother and I are aging and I expected you to be our support, you being our only son.

Yet...."

Rohit's mother *(in tears)* - "Uff... Could you please let it go? It was just a bad dream!

There's no point in scolding him!"

"Thank god it was just a dream Naina!!

Had it been a reality, we wouldn't have got a second chance!

What's appalling is that your son could actually think of something like this!

All this while he never realized that he was sedated and he simply kept on blabbering; without realizing how much his words were infuriating me!

Nothing could've been done while he was in his slumber; but now...

Adarsh and all are also here and...

...Doesn't is bother you to know that he was planning to kill himself?

Rohit's father turned away in disgust and fury.

He tried to speak out his frustration but then realized that the presence of his family and Rohit's friends didn't make it a perfect setting for that to happen; so he gnashed his teeth as hard as he could.

For him Rohit was his strong lad in whom he held great pride.

Even the very thought of his son taking away his own life had brought him to a state of extreme delirium which he was unable to express.

Meanwhile Rohit eluded the vehemence of his father in his mother's arms; who kept rubbing her son's arm as he shivered in pain and fear.

Rohit failed to understand how fantasies and veridicalities had coalesced into one...

Meanwhile...

Abhay- "Bang on Adarsh!

Your guess was right!

It is Pragya!"

Adarsh *(rustling into Abhay's ear)* - "Ssshh…. Uncle is mad at him… At least don't bring up that topic right now!"

"Don't Ssshh me, I had a stake for a hundred with Karan on this; and to be precise, it is more of my victory that it is yours!"

Karan-"Abhay… I'll give you two hundred Abhay; but please, shut up!"

Abhay-"Profit! Profit! Profit! Ha-ha!

Oops!

Ok! I'll be quiet!"

All eyes were on Abhay!

And Abhay…he soon realized that no one was in the mood to caper!

Rohit overheard this light conversation but never gestured the fact.

Hitherto, his friends remained silent spectators and no one, especially Abhay sought it to be a good idea to speak.

There was a brief period of silence which then filled the room.

Rohit- "Papa, I... I really don't know how all of this happened!

How can one have control over his dreams?"

"Rohit this wasn't a normal dream! This was a lucid one.

You had been tranquilized yet you were still aware of the fact that Adarsh, Karan and Abhay were present in the room!

Your dreams depicted nothing except what you could have done in reality!

You were conversing with them in reality...

Your vision was nothing but a mockery of truth and fiction!"

"Not at all Papa... Ma and you mean the world to me.

I simply cannot agree that it was a lucid dream!

If there's anything that's true in this world then it is the fact that I worship you more than I adore you!

Yes...I did fall weak when you had denied persuading Pragya's father any further but...

When I reflect on what I had thought of doing, I pity myself!

I'm sorry!"

Rohit's father *(interrupting)* - "... At least we could've talked over it before you had started thinking of doing such stupid stuff!

Bly me; if you hadn't been admitted in the ICCU; I would have seriously slapped you out of your dream!

What hasn't your dad done for you!

Tell me Rohit, where have I not supported you?

You could've come up to me and spoken about it!

We could've found a solution!

And I mean come on, who doesn't have a crush in life?
Even I had one...

She was an infatuation and to be fair it was both sided!

But, spending lives together is something way more serious.

I was always ready to have a talk with Pragya's father, but...

If persuasion is what you ask of me; it will be done beta!

But, you simply can't give up!

You got to make lemonade from the lemons that life throws at you rather than repenting on the fact that you couldn't have a glass of wine!

I never went on to inquire anything about her but, if there were any debates which compared her religion or caste to that of ours; our battles were already won!

...And even if it hadn't been so; I would've been okay with it, coz classifying humans into religions or nationalities is what muggins do!

Love doesn't care of social barriers and not only love, but for the sake of humanity, it's really important that it's humanism that should be accepted as a religion.

The classification of people into religions or nationalities is simply a way of creating differences.

If her father isn't willing to consider the person whom she loves, you should give it a damn.

She had tried at her end, but if her father wouldn't listen, do you really think that your plan to end your life would actually help that cause?

Do you?

… And if she is accepting her father's decision what excuses you to not to follow mine?

I can't go and force him…

It's his daughter's life and he has complete authority to take any decision that he deems correct.

If Pragya really loves you; she should be the one fighting for you rather than you begging for consideration!

Crying over spilled milk isn't a solution Rohit!

Perhaps, your destiny has something better in store for you.

And- you are MY SON!!

You can't give up… At least not like this…"

"But Papa, it's a matter of two lives!

I… I…I could perhaps still be able to manage living without her but, I just can't allow her to not to revolt against her father's conservative mind.

There's this voice that comes from my heart Papa.

It talks to me and tells me, 'She's the one!'

I can't let her go away papa.

She's scared of speaking out in front of her parents.

Imagine the purity of her innocence which prevents her from standing up and speaking her heart out in front of her parents.

I have to do something for her Papa... And it's not a matter of only two lives.

If we don't end up being together, then, our so called future life partners will also be affected by this decision.

Rohit's father gave a stony stare.

Rohit's mother- "Beta... Enough! If the doctor, finds out that you have been stressing yourself immediately after regaining consciousness; he will drive all of us out of this room!

The visiting hours will be over soon!

We can discuss all of it later on...

But first, you need to get well!"

Rohit did understand what his mother tried to tell him but some things at that time were more important than his own well-being!

He wasn't sure of his sentiency and wanted to make the most of the opportunity that he had got!

"Papa-I guess I should let you know that when all of this was taking place Pragya had called me and told me that if she was married to somebody else then that person would only be only using her body.

She went on to say that by not being with me; she would be dead within and that there would be no love in her marriage.

She would merely be a person who had started living in some other house doing the household work over there and simply sleeping with some other man.

What do you expect me to do when I hear such words from the likes of her?"

Rohit's father got agitated with the level of frankness that his son had shared with him.

His voice rose like a rested lion, pouncing on its prey to quench its disturbia...

"Rohit, I agree that I consider you my friend. But you have to understand that there are certain things that should be kept strictly between the two of you.

I've been of your age and I understand what falling in love is like!

You needn't explain to me about all that...

And once again, I'm trying to get this in your head that falling in love and spending lives with each other are things which are totally different from each other!

Why don't you take her as a song which was never yours...?

Yet, whenever you sang it; it helped you express all your emotions!

Why don't you take her as your friend who's been something which is in excess of the definition of the word 'friendship' itself?

It could be love, but, is love all about ageing together?

Doesn't sacrifice refer to a form of love?

I have been a friend to you and will always be.

But, at the same time, by being your father, I would also like to tell you that tying a knot to love isn't victory.

Sometimes, you have to let go of the birds.

They'll be yours only if they fly back to you.

Caging them doesn't make them yours...

And one more thing; always respect the intimacy Pragya shares with you..."

Adarsh, Karan and Abhay thought that it was not such a good time for them to be present in the room anymore.

They were undoubtedly concerned for their childhood friend but, at the same time they also thought that it was necessary for them to leave Rohit to his parents' company!

Moreover, if they hadn't made a voluntary decision; the ending visiting hours would've surely made them take one!

Things; off late; had been moving quite fast to their liking.

Absorbing the quantum of changes that had been brought about in their lives was something they found very difficult to cope with.

A few days ago Rohit was down with high fever because of which they had come to visit him!

And today, out of nowhere they had gained the knowledge of their friend's affaire!

Rohit was now; actually having a conversation with his dad regarding him getting married to the girl with whom he was in love...

A love story that had never been spoken of!

A tale that had been a well-kept secret for quite some time!

Rohit- the Magicman had fallen in love.

Back in school, he was the one who would keep laughing in disbelief when asked to form an opinion regarding when he would get married!

And now... all of it seemed a lie!

As Rohit's friends left the room; Rohit tried making an eye contact.

...and once he did, he passed on a tired smile which acknowledged his indebtedness because of the concern shown by his pals...

Suddenly the room seemed to have become more spacious than what it was a few moments ago!

Silence had perhaps got more room to fill itself in.

And amidst these, Rohit tried expressing his mentation:

"Papa I'm sorry...

The only reason I shared my thoughts with you is to make you realize how badly I love her!

It didn't mean anything else!"

Echoes of his voice reverbed in the room!

There was resonance in his speech which caught the immediate attention of his parents; who had diverted his attention to bid adieu to Rohit's friends!

Rohit's father immediately reacted to the words addressed to him and went on to say:

"Your willingness to give away your life for her clearly states your feeling towards her.

Now, be brave and fight like a man.

Behave like you are your father's son and face the situation!

I will do all that's possible for you because, something that makes my son happy is something I strive for.

Leave it to me.

But, you have to promise that no matter what be the outcome you are going to accept it like a strong and matured man!

Swear that you'll not even think of committing yourself to something stupid!"

"I swear Papa- I won't disappoint you!

But what will you do?

Her father wouldn't even consider me!

He's not at all interested in having a talk with you!

He..."

"If the problem is with her dad, let your dad deal with him!

If he thinks he can stick to his stupid laws of conservatism I will show him that being friends with children and having an open mind isn't hazardous."

"But what are you going to do?

Papa- I'm scared!

Please tell me...

I want to know how you are going to deal with the entire situation!"

".... Naina, is he really my son? Do something to make him stronger!

And you....Arrange me Pragya's father's number and leave the rest on me."

"Are you going to call him now?"

Rohit's father narrowed his vision and smiled.

The only words that came out of his mouth as he looked at his son were:

"Rohit...Never... Never... Never give up...!"

Lions roar a solemn song
Victors speak of an oblivious dong
A hero falls to the shades of night
Glories lost in a moment's blight
Expectations bowing down the shoulders
Stringent roads with in numerous boulders
And amidst these the heart
jolts a thumping sound
Never give in- Never give up- the
game goes on another round

Eagles caged in a petty arraign
Mindless critics praise, what others gain!
Blood and dust blend into ane
Companies lost which once swore to sustain
Vivacious lights fade away
Leaving all hopes in complete disarray
And amidst these the heart
jolts a thumping sound
Never give in- Never give up- the
game goes on another round

Acinonyxs stare a voluptuous affair
Plenty to blame and no one to care
Gathering themselves, the fallen rise
Queering the worldly thoughts
to their bosom's suffice
Isolated in disgust, harking a swanking roar
Another trial before conflating in the galore

And amidst these the heart
jolts a thumping sound
Never give in- Never give up- the
game goes on another round

Sapiens challenge in abundance and ask
'What's left of thou who are
obscured and masked?'
But the hero doesn't answer,
nor does he scream
Standing tall he mends ways to be seen
Lathering all over, he never sleeps
Hollering blood- he never weeps
And amidst these the heart
jolts a thumping sound
Never give in- Never give up- Own
the game in this very round

Perspiration fills into a glass of wine
What's felt is heavenly, sultrous yet divine
Tears fill in firm detritus eyes
Vanquishing temporal voices beheld as lies
Not for glory- Not for fame
But for the sake of keeping the champ's name
The heart jolts a thumping sound
Never give in- Never give up- Arrogate
triumph on every pound

Chapter 4

Tale of the Boondocks

"In order to consider someone for marriage, love must exist between the two, and this cannot happen without being friends with the person.

You must know the person.

You must know his or her habits…you must know his or her temper… you must know his or her principles…you just… you must know the person.

You cannot love a person without knowing that person.

So this calls for friendship before marriage.

Based on that knowledge, we either love a person or not.

If friendship feels right, then love shall definitely flow in to our hearts!"

-Pak Quran

*S*ome parents always proclaim that they treat all their children as equals, but, truth be told, no matter how much they love them; there's always a bit of disparity amongst them; either on the basis of their sex, age or interests and capabilities/incapabilities.

There can be many reasons to this differentiation but, the fact prevails that people decorate their acts in such a way that they try to make it believe that equality amongst their children always sustains; which as a matter of fact is nothing but an ornamented lie.

The truth is that no two children are loved equally. The very reason behind this is that love can never be measured. It is the situations that we are put into; in our lives which decide how we should react.

Love is immeasurable. Love can never be quantified. Love can never be compared. Each and every relation, in its own way, is unique and special.

Another thing that also needs to be understood is that there's a big difference between being educated and that of being qualified and to be true, if one *appraises the difference between the two, then, the rarity of the existence of the educated would soon be realized.*

If people were actually educated, then questions on the age old intellects of the society would've definitely been raised.

Yet, these norms are rarely questioned; never reasoned; hardly argued and are on most occasions; accepted in the solace of good faith.

Our acts, on various instances, are somewhat an adaptation of an upbringing modified to fit in the modern era.

Compromises are found in abundance and the quantum of love diminishes with practical priorities ranking high.

It indeed is the bourgeois or the middle class which pays the highest price to this vandalism.

Though the effluxion of time has bought about a number of changes in the way people think and in the way people react; but, these changes are nothing but mere adjustments to the modern lifestyle.

Rarely people have had the time to question the happenings around them.

Perhaps; because on a numerous occasions; they are either caught up with their work or do not consider the turn of events to be their cup of tea.

People believe that times have changed and with it, they've become more open-minded but; the truth can never be done away with.

Within each and every individual trapped in the societal structure; there is a corner of the heart which seeks comfort; which seeks settling down; which seeks a reason to escape to the land of dreams!

And for this very reason it is a patron to change only to find a peaceful accommodation in its fauna.

Both, Pragya and Rohit were a part of this very social structure, yet, a huge difference existed between the setups of their family positions.

Rohit's aimed and attaining aristocracy whereas Pragya's aspired to the asseveration of the bourgeoisie.

Moreover, since Pragya was the eldest amongst her four sisters, her father couldn't simply ignore his slavery to bourgeoisie before he had actually accepted Rohit's proposal.

There were certainly no major negatives in accepting Rohit as a groom to his eldest daughter.

None at all!

But for a father who had been buttoned down with prejudicial societal principles, it wasn't always an easy decision for him to make.

Had Pragya been the youngest of all his daughters, this wouldn't have been a ponderable theme of thought!

However, leaving aside Pragya, he had to cater the responsibility of three more daughters and considering all this he needed time to think.... He needed some time before he could arrive at a conclusion.

Children, however, under such circumstances, never understand the underlying matter which drives the factual conversations.

Cupid often weakens the power of practicality and the true meaning of the ornamental words is hardly interpreted.

Where experience teaches the true meaning of the words coined to fill in the situation; there, on the other hand; youth remains an ally to lexicon!

After Rohit's father had had a conversation with Pragya's father, Pragya's family felt as if it had been kissed by the tempest!

There were queries; questions; perceptions; theories... All lining up against her!

...And to all of it, she had no answer!

She wanted to talk to Rohit regarding everything that had been going on at her place. Even though her parents had not permitted her to talk to any of her male friends without seeking their permission she urged to disobey so that she could bring peace to her heart.

Somehow, she managed to access her confiscated cell phone at three in the morning, when everyone was asleep.

Whispering and whimpering; words painted in her voice fell on Rohit's desperate ears.

"Rohit... Hi!

How are you?"

She sobbed.

It was this unusual noise that she made as she spoke; that brought a scintillation of goose bumps on Rohit's skin.

A perfect mixture of happiness blended in grief!

Rohit was more lost in her voice than on the thought as to what he had to speak next!

He was almost done with his reciprocation before which Pragya continued to speak:

"... Rohit! There are a few things that I would like to tell you. I don't know from where I should begin; but ever since my father has had a talk with your father; you have been the center of discussion o'er here.

...From dinner table conversations; to tea-time chats to late night confluences... You're the one who's being talked of!

I'm nervous..."

She paused for a while.

Long and appeasing breaths accompanied her silence.

This silence, however, was intensely discomforting for Rohit who had been lurking to wipe it out.

"What talks?

Are they good or bad?"

"I don't know Rohit!

Hardly am I allowed to be a participant in any of these conversations that have been taking place!

It has now been more than a month since I was last allowed to leave my room.

Nevertheless, somehow, I have managed to overhear their confabulations!

And to be honest with you...The biggest fear; that bothers my father is that he doesn't know your family!

Rohit, there are no shortcomings regarding you. As a matter of fact, my dad has been inquiring of you and your family and..."

"I hope that whatever he has come to know of us, is good!"

"That's the thing Rohit... Everything about you is a bit too good to his liking!"

"Is that supposed to be a problem?"

Silence seeped in yet again.

Pragya lost track of her train of thought that she had adopted for corroborating her mind.

Somehow, she successfully attempted at elusively narrating the scheme of events and went on to elaborate the situation in which her family had placed itself.

"Rohit...there's a lot of history to my family!

Even though you are aware of everything concerning my past, there are a few things that I haven't told you of; even now!

These issues don't involve me but, I'm getting a feeling that they might be one of the major factors influencing my father's decision..."

"I'm listening baby..."

"The youngest of my mother's sisters; who was ten years elder to me had also fallen in love while she was in college!

This was something completely unacceptable to my grandparents. My aunt didn't know what she could do to win their hearts so she decided to elope with the guy with whom she had fallen in love with.

They ran away and got married.

The maternal side of my family was completely against this.

They tried parting with her on all grounds but things aren't always as seemingly when spoken.

The love for the blood of thy own can never be undone and eventually, after the initial hassle; everybody had to accept her love!

For my aunt, it was a fairy tale that was being scripted into reality.

She was happy!

Her husband was very caring...He loved her a lot.

Their family prospered like anything post marriage and some where my grandparents started feeling that they had been wrong for not having accepted her marriage in the first place."

"If this is the story that is influencing your father's decision, I guess I have nothing to be worried about."

"This isn't the end of the story Rohit. There's a bit more to it than you think.

Every relationship has this initial phase of being gaga about each other.

Everyone always puts their best foot forward in a relationship at the beginning!

It's always good to know a person and fall in love with that person. But, remaining in love with that same person for the rest of the life is the biggest challenge.

My aunt and her husband were like two best friends who had been given the prosperous destiny to spend the rest of their lives with each other! Everything was picturesque.

The caring, sharing, laughing and loving.... All of it!

But with time, my aunt had to blend in as a member of the family. Her husband started to realize that she was nothing but an outcast to his family.

Once the fever of being newlywed subsided he agnized that my aunt didn't match the standards to fit into his family!

149

There was this difference of class between the two that had struck him all of a sudden.

I mean, all this while this never happened to have existed but out of nowhere he started feeling that he had got married a bit too early!

He started behaving as if he owned her...

And she; She was like a spider that was caught in its own web! Helpless; incapacitated; lost in the bewilderment of relationships!

Her husband's bossism was initially a control issue.

However, with the passage of time he started eliminating her friends and family from their lives and made her completely boycott her social life.

Auntie always wondered in confusedness to this strange behavior of his. To be honest, she was still trying to understand why her husband had changed all of a sudden!

She needed a reason because the man with whom she had been living lately wasn't the person with whom she had fallen in love with.

It was her free-spirited self which was something her husband loved the most but, once they were married he had started dominating her in every single way that can be thought of!

And the saddest part about all of it was that, once my aunt was made to abandon all her social relations; people distanced from her; which all of us now realize; was her husband's main objective!

Somewhere, this dark side of him took over his sanity and he started treating her like an object.

At first; he wasn't all that comfortable in introducing her to his colleagues. Later on; a time came when he started introducing her as his bitch!"

"Baby...! I understand how this entire story is being related to us but we've been together for a while now!

Am I really that kind of a person?

Is it fair that whatever your father has experienced be compared with everything that comes his way as of now?

"...Rohit! I... I...I really don't... It's a catch-22 for me Rohit!

It really is..."

"There's so many a taboo that.... Are all of them comparable?"

"They aren't Rohit...they absolutely aren't!

But... please understand my dilemma!

I... I think there is something else apart from all that I've told you till now that has been bothering my father!

He has had a lot of discussions with all the elders in the family regarding some issues of which I have no clue.

But I think I know what it could've been!

"Sure... Sure...I'd really wanna know why!"

"Once my grandparents had accepted the marriage; the in-laws of their other children and society at large started gossips involving them.

Some people asked them indirectly; how much money had they given as dowry; coz the family in which my aunt was married held a very high societal position when compared to theirs.

A few, on the other hand, rumored that my aunt had become pregnant before marriage and that the marriage was just a way of covering things up.

Things weren't easy for them. They had to face a lot of things; which they gallantly did.

What the society thought of them was never regarded by them. They always did something which bought happiness to their family.

But when all these incidents started happening with their youngest daughter, the voice of the society started resonating in their ears.

They entire scheme of events was heartrending for them.

That bastard started beating up my aunt almost on a daily basis. He would get drunk and return home late every night and once he did so; he would then start his tantrums.

He would rape her and then start to abuse her in the filthiest manners possibly known.

A shiver is sent down my spine each time I think o'er it...

There was a little pause after which Pragya continued:

He used to keep her tied with nylon ropes; used to pull her by her hair and beat her in places where the bruises would never come up!

Her ribs had been broken quite a number of times!

She had to dress herself in such a way that she could cover her bruises.

Her life was miserable, but because she started fearing her husband she never dared to go and speak about her private life in public.

Whenever she met any of her family members, she would manage to keep a smile on her face and not let anybody know the truth behind her smile.

All of this went on for quite a long time.

Auntie was shamed; humiliated; degraded; tortured in ways beyond our imagination.

We were shell-shocked when we came to know that her day used to begin by being thrown out of the bed which had been turned upside down.

It was by an accident that my grandfather had come to know of this torture that her most adorned daughter was a subject to!

But once he did come to know of it; he along with my father helped her file a divorce suit against that person and help her move out of his house.

...Getting out of that house was a breather for her but the vandalism of that man did not end o'er there.

He couldn't accept the fact that the person whom he had started treating as his bitch had left him and left him for good!

So he started following her to places.

He started teasing her.

Calling her names...

Started making rumors of my aunt having an extra marital affair with some other guy and what not!

To keep things in control, we had to get a restraining order from the court! And after the passage of a long period of time things finally came into place!

But, the end result to all of it was that...

...The end result to all of it was that my aunt's spirit had been taken away from her.

She had lost her soul!

She had lost a lot in life!

She was a very jovial person from what I remember of her, but when she returned to our family she was a completely different person! She had changed....

And that wasn't all; that destiny had in store for her...

There was perhaps some good that was still left for her!

There was this angel who was really commoved with her struggle and after all this; he had decided to marry her for the brave heart she had been and the person she was.

Though auntie had forgotten how to laugh; forgotten how to smile; forgotten how to live... She never forgot humanity!"

"Isn't that a bit too much to digest given your aunt's situation?

Didn't that person think over all these issues?"

"He did... he did put in a lot of thinking.

But after the death of his first wife at an early age, he had been looking for a mother to his young daughter when he happened to have met my aunt!

One could say that he was more in search of a mother to his daughter than for a wife for himself. But, honestly speaking whatever may be the initial reason...

... I guess it is something that shouldn't be thought for long.

Perhaps, because they were a perfect match to each other!

Both the families belonged to the same class and adjusting to the family culture wasn't a demanding task for my aunt either.

They were happy...happily married and they also had a child... Whom they had named 'Tamanna' which meant hope!

A hope of life..."

"...Tamanna?"

"Yes Rohit; Tamanna!"

"So...?"

"Yes... This is the reason why I always told you that if we ever had a daughter in the future we would name her Tamanna!"

"Wow! That's beautiful!"

Pragya hinted a smile...

Though this was something which wasn't vocally audible, Rohit had heard it with an elaborated ease.

Four years from when Tamanna was born; my aunt started experiencing lumps on her body, which had been causing her a lot of pain for quite some time.

Thus, for the peace of her mind she consulted this with her primary care physician and scheduled a biopsy.

...And when the results did come out, it was as if her nightmares had disguised themselves into something different!

She was diagnosed of Stage-IV Breast Cancer."

"Oh God...!"

"She fought against it for the next ten years of her life!

It was then when I realized that people in general are hopeful and always like talking about positive stuff!

They like giving themselves hope...

Any why shouldn't they?

If hope can save lives, I guess everybody would like to hope that everything will be alright!

Having seen her fight against cancer gave everybody in our family a lot of hope!

Things started looking better after innumerous sessions of chemotherapy!

There was this feeling that she was going to be one of those breast cancer survivors who would become a protagonist to the many suffering from the same disease; but...

Rohit; she fought a lot... The best she could fight... The kind of fight she always had with her life...

But, she finally lost the war... Many of the battles were hers' for the taking but at last she had to succumb herself to death!

She passed away...!

... She passed away last year, Rohit!

She's no more with us..."

Having said this, Pragya went quiet! Rohit, on the other hand, needed words with which he could kill the silence that had become a major reason of discomfort!

He was hesitant yet somehow went on to speak:

"I...I... I'm...I'm so sorry to hear that!

I really don't know what to say!

I'm at loss for words!

May her soul rest in peace..."

A period of noiselessness came up yet again.

No one hung up on the other. Both, Pragya and Rohit could hear each other breathe o'er the phone.

There was a wave of inarticulateness, quiescence and sullenness in the air!

What kept the moment alive were gasps of air from two individuals involved in a moot duration!

Then... all of a sudden, the captivating silence was shredded by a feminine voice smudged in languishment:

"Considering all that I've gone through and the status that your family has; my father fears that history is being repeated!

My mom has started making conclusions that considering your family's background and your acceptance of me; even after knowing all that I've been through hints that there might be something putrid about you and your family that hasn't been revealed."

"... Is that so?

Pragya, I do respect you a lot, and even though I am appalled on having heard what has happened with your mother's sister; please think over it... Is it justified to think that everybody on this planet is the same?

Does history actually repeat itself on all instances?"

"It isn't justified Rohit!

It absolutely isn't.

But I have got no role to play in these decisions!

My mother has a free mind and she can think of whatever comes to her mind.

I can't stop her from doing that!

I simply can't!

All I'm doing is just letting you know what she has been thinking off-late!

She's stern because she knows what it's like to be weak.

She keeps a guard because she knows what it's like to; having cried her to sleep.

This is the reason why she's like this!

There's nothing against you!

Nothing...

In fact, my mother has been inquisitive to know more about you, ever since my father has had a talk with your father.

She has accessed Facebook using my profile and has browsed through each and every photograph of yours; that you've uploaded.

The look on her face while doing so was noteworthy!

It was as if she was churned up on having seen your photographs!"

"...churned up...! Why?"

"I don't have an answer to that Rohit!

There is something that has been bothering her.

She wants to see you and since then she has been devising a plan on how that can happen!"

"So...what's the problem with that?

We can always plan a meeting as per her convenience and she can clear whatever doubts that she has in her mind regarding me!

Can't we?"

The entire conversation had heated up Rohit's cell phone; therefore, making him, swap his hearing ear. And as soon as he did so, he went on to hear Pragya speak:

"...The thing is that she doesn't want to meet you Rohit.

In fact, what she has been planning is to go and check you out from a distance while you're at work."

"That's fine by me! But..."

"Rohit; I don't know if I should tell you this but, there have been things that I've been pointed out as well and I... I..."

"Whatever it is; please speak out Pragya!"

There was a considerable amount of hesitation on the other end.

Sometimes it's important that certain talks are kept within the family.

But, the thing with being in love is that people often share quiet a lot... A lot than what's actually required!

And as the saying goes; the excess of anything can be injurious to health; so it is for relationships as well!

"...While mama was having a look at some of your pictures; she proclaimed that you looked like an abuse to mankind!

According to her; there was nothing attractive about you that should've made me fall in love with you...

I know you're a great person, but..."

"Hang on!

...You agreed with her?

The world has complete authority to conceive perceptions. I give a damn to what the world thinks of me!

But it really hurts when the person whom I love the most sticks up a 'but' during such a conversation!"

"... Rohit; I did stand for you!

I did stand up against my mother on this ground, but, there's a limit to which I could revolt!

I just can't deny my mother's decree!"

"Why can't you?"

"...Coz that's disrespecting!"

"That's not disrespecting, that's being correct!

You have the right to live your life independently being a woman of this generation.

I understand whatever that has happened with your mother's sister has made her more protective of you, but, I don't think that this is the way things should be dealt with!

If your mother stops you from doing so, I don't expect you to have a fight with her and win a conversation.

They are our elders, and we, being their children, should never raise our voices against them, no matter how big a disadvantage comes our way.

I agree it is very difficult on our part to eradicate the views that have bogged down their minds over the generations, but, we have to take small steps; one at a time, to bring in reason in the way everybody thinks!"

"You may give it by whatever reason you wish to Rohit, but things are always easier said than done.

... All that I've managed at my end is that, instead of my mother; it'll be Sweta who'll be coming to meet you!

My mother will be using her as bait and will be standing at a distance to see you while you have a conversation with Sweta.

I've wangled hard to make this call just so that you don't feel cheated when this happens!"

Then she thought of the scheme of things; and tried wrapping up the conversation...

"Rohit, I think my mother is waking up so I'll have to disconnect the call.

Just to give you a heads up, Sweta is very tech savvy. If you've got to impress her you've got to play the cards right. So don't forget bringing your sedan when you meet her.

Please take care of yourself!

Love you.

Bye"

Rohit- "Hello…"

Before Rohit could speak any further the call had been disconnected.

He kept trying to call her but Pragya's cell phone had been switched off.

What, according to Pragya, was a conversation that had reached its conclusion was something with which Rohit wasn't completely satisfied.

He had a lot to speak out but, the uncomfortable feeling he had could be kept only to his loneliness.

He pondered over the conversation and sought a way in which he could express himself. Suddenly, he saw his laptop and realized that there was perhaps a way by which he could do so.

And so, in sheer desperation he grabbed hold of his laptop and started banging the keypad. He was doing something which he wasn't supposed to do. Not unless he had informed Pragya about it. But, there wasn't any other option which he could think of being possible.

Prateek Surana

Beyond the darkness of the night
Silent winds cross the bounded
humane desires
Entombed in a city known to the loved
The dreams are haunted by those
doomed for an eternity
And lust lures its usurious wings o'er me
As I build a dream from mere vicinity
And my beloved, now that you're here
Allowing me to sink in your arms
I pledge my soul, I pledge my poetry
Never judge a person by way of his looks
If you can't but, feel the inner beauty

Lust and anger are siblings for long ago
And revenge or beauty may come and go
But true love lasts till the end
Repelling the thought that consumes your head
A servant to your heart
The chalice of your love a lustful necrophilia
And my beloved, now that you're here
Allowing me to sink in your arms
I pledge my soul, I pledge my poetry
Never judge a person by way of his looks
If you can't but, feel the inner beauty

Happy Holidays!

Like the wings of a bird of prey
Love shadowed o'er me till the brink of day
Drowning in the never ending sea of your eyes
I search for my destiny, I search for a life
Don't walk away as the world burns on me
A fortress falls turning into ash gratis
And my beloved, now that you're here
Allowing me to sink in your arms
I pledge my soul, I pledge my poetry
Never judge a person by way of his looks
If you can't but, feel the inner beauty

The whispers of truth second
the silence of trust
Mythologizing the long luring lust
And treasures now stolen from your dream
Gossips lost in a heart which can't scream
Gazing into the cerulean lazuline lonely sky
Praying for a cosmos to the bosom's suffice
And my beloved, now that you're here
Allowing me to sink in your arms
I pledge my soul, I pledge my poetry
Never judge a person by way of his looks
If you can't but, feel the inner beauty

Prateek Surana

Important

Hi Sweta,

First of all, I don't know why I'm writing this mail! But I guess, given the situation, this was the best way I could've expressed myself. It is an earnest request that you keep this conversation strictly between the two of us rather than telling about it to everybody. I expect that the information I am going to share with you might make things more clear.

1. Pragya and I have known each other for donkey's ears. I have always supported her in all her endeavors.

2. Pragya too has a lot of pictures on Facebook. But, I ask you, is it really fair to judge people on the basis of their looks? I've known Pragya and have loved her for her good nature and for the person that she is. Never have I or have allowed anybody to judge her on her looks! Yet, this is totally my point of view that a person should never be judged by his/her looks.

3. I can't comment on how good or bad I am; but, the last conversation that I had with your sister has been excruciatingly painful for me. I have made honest attempts to suffice all the needs that a woman would want to have in her future life partner; but somewhere down the line, I find her too submissive to your parents coz she just can't speak up to them. Sweta, I do understand the problems she is facing, yet what I expect of her is to be brave and speak up for the special bond that we share.

I once again request you to not to bring up anything regarding this mail. This mail is strictly meant for you so that you may know how it feels being at the receiving end. Please support her through adverse situations.

From the deepest core of my heart, I have truly and genuinely loved your sister.

Please make things happen. I am counting on you to help us through!

Rohit

Re: Important

Hey Rohit,

Yes...I have received your mail and have read through all that you wanted to convey!

... And it's not how you're taking things to be.

She was audacious enough to speak to my parents regarding you.

Papa has been eager ever-since! As far as your looks are concerned, she had also gone on to say that you were the best looking person in the world for her.

My parents have confiscated her cell phone because they feel that it is not virtuous to talk to boys about marriage and I don't think that they are wrong!

After all; it is extremely important for a girl to stay within the limit of her compliance!

On roads where villains walk with pride
I'll use the devil to be my guide
Crippled by the boundaries of mankind
I shan't program myself to guilt
Lest my nerves; they start to tilt

I sit in a room of mirrors
Watching the distance continue for miles
Yet everything in there is a sham
Fooling me with is lustful Instagram
Every word I uttered
And every thought I had
The good, the medieval or the bad

It is nothing but an avenue of
sinners where I'm employed
Having to work there till I myself am destroyed
Static as the stone thrown in the river
I never moved till the earth made me quiver
A signal received which for long I ignored
I rose again to prove the worth
of my umbilical cord
Haunted by experiences of the
past troubling me from inside
Breaking all barriers that kept
me away from being alive

Happy Holidays!

Before the undertaker drives the last nail
Into the coffin where I shall oddment all pains
A reason to cherish my life
A reason to smile I shall find
A reason; I shall find for them
to remember my name
A reason; I shall find to feel alive once again!

Chapter 5

The Bachelors'

"The destruction of our kindred means the destruction of the -traditions of our ancient lineage, and when these are lost, irreligion will overrun our homes.

When irreligion spreads, the women of the house begin to stray; when they lose their purity, adulteration of the stock follows.

Promiscuity ruins both the family and those who defile it; while the souls of our ancestors droop, through lack of the funeral cakes and ablutions.

By the destruction of our lineage and the pollution of blood, ancient class traditions and family purity alike perish.

Alas, it is strange that we should be willing to kill our own countrymen and commit a great sin, in order to enjoy the pleasures of a kingdom."

-The Bhagwat Gita

*S*ometimes dreams are nothing but a persistent reality and when one is in love, falling asleep isn't really an option because finally... Finally the reality is something which is better than the dream!

But, what also needs to be understood is that sometimes reality can be nothing but, a mere illusion; an enchanted spell, which the mind refuses to accept.

Dreams can never be turned into reality lest we actually wake up-Lest we actually rise.

A child is never taught how to love, how to dream or how to believe. These things don't differentiate the rich and the poor. They simply flash in our minds and leave imprints on our imagination.

It takes only a minute to get a crush on someone; an hour to like someone; and a day to love someone. But, it takes a lifetime to forget someone!

And amidst this, hope plays an integral part.

The heart will always love and the mind will always keep dreaming. That's life!

And the way Rohit intended to live his life was that he had never stopped hoping. No matter how hard were the circumstances; he always believed in following something which his heart believed was true...

A fight against conservatism was something which isn't all that easy, especially when it was being advocated by a person who had complete authority over the love of his life. However, after a series of indirect conversations with Pragya's father, Rohit somehow was able to convey his mentation to Pragya's father who finally met him and his father.

Nevertheless, the traits of conservatism can never be done away with completely. It indeed is funny that people often talk about gender equality; but, when families of the conservative mind place themselves in such situations; it is the man who is expected to take the initiating step on most occasions!

To be fair to both the sexes, Rohit's father had an equal right to know the person whom his son had chosen as his proposed life-partner! But, conservatism has its exorbitant wings shaded all over feminism and Pragya or perhaps her family sought this as a perfect excuse to avoid her presence in this interaction.

The concourse however, did leave smiles on all faces!

Things were going great for Rohit and Pragya.

Perhaps exactly the way they had dreamt it to be.

After the incomplete conversation that Rohit had had with Pragya, he had been desperate to talk to her. But, after having met her father; he actually didn't bother much on the fact that his conversations with her were yet to be completed.

The only reason behind this being that somewhere; deep within his heart he had started feeling that Pragya was his...

For a girl who belongs to a conservative family, speaking her heart out is perhaps the most difficult task. There are, perhaps, innumerous thoughts which she would like to express yet; somewhere all of it is buried inside her heart just so that she can be a good daughter.

And the harsh truth about reality is that silence is often termed as an acceptance!

No matter what be the decision; many a time voices can't be raised!

Some call it giving respect; some term it as the fear of their elders. Whatever may be the reason; the truth is that the voices of individuality are somewhere lost amidst all this!

The heart is a stupid fool. It never mends its ways!

It was, is and shall always be free spirited! Falling in love is something it decides and that is something that can never be controlled!

Rohit knew all of what was on Pragya's mind and he was finally foreseeing a positive end to his fairy-tale-Spending lives together; growing old with her best friend and having the opportunity to share the ups and downs of life with someone; in whose company he found himself to be angelic!

It was a moment of rejoice and perhaps the best time for him to attend the bachelors' night of one of his closest friends.

The occasion was staged at a night club in a hotel, where, both Rohit and Adarsh found the balcony to be the best place for them to hang out. They lazed on the rocking chairs placed in the balcony!

Silence had been prevailing for quite a long time between the two, which was suddenly broken by a random question raised by Adarsh:

"So Mr. Magicman, when do I get to attend your bachelors'?"

Rohit remained silent for some time and then broke the silence with a puff of air, followed by the words that then came out of his mouth:

"Tell me something bro!

Am I an abuse to mankind?

I mean, I do understand everything that has been going on off-late but...

Confusion appeared on Adarsh's face! Unaware of the reasons behind Rohit's sudden outburst, he kept staring at him trying to figure out a reason...

I don't know how I can convey what has been going on my mind brother!

Things have been complicated!

Things have been irritatingly frivolous!

I fail to understand why!

Just when I thought that everything was falling in place; Pragya sends me an email; telling me that what we had was nothing but a dream!

'All dreams come to an end'- she said! So was our dream of being together!

Each attempt that I make in trying to understand the scheme of events; more helpless do I find myself!

Why do things have to be so complicated?

Why can't things be simpler than what they are?

I loved her and so did she... then why all of this?

Rohit then took out his cell phone and made Adarsh read the mail that Pragya had sent him so that it would be easier for him to explain how the entire episode had fared.

Very Important

Hi,

Rohit, please forgive me.

I wanted to tell you something but as my cell phone has been confiscated I have somehow managed to use the internet and am writing you this mail!

Rohit, off late papa hasn't been well and for the past few days he has been crying himself to sleep! Neither can my mom control her tears! They are cursing themselves for having given birth to me.

Rohit please forgive me but I can't marry you. You are a clean soul and I know you have always cared and respected me, that's why I am begging you to forget me.

Please don't pursue any further.

My father won't be able to bear it.

If something happens to him, my entire family will be destroyed.

You are my best friend, and will always be…and for the sake of our friendship, promise me that you won't tell anything about our relationship to my father. He has been living on medicines.

You always told me that nothing would ever happen without my parent's permission. Thus, for the sake of my father; please forgive me!

All my self-respect is now in your hands. Please don't let me fall any further in the eyes of my father. He hasn't been talking to me. Don't let anybody know about our relationship! I guess it's not correct of me to tell you this coz you worship me and respect me. My father just couldn't bear with the fact that his daughter had dared to fall in love!

All of this is having a toll on my sisters as well. Please rectify all that has happened. Please give me one more chance so that I can rise in the eyes of my father once again.

Please fulfill this last request of your best friend.

Pragya

Rohit smiled in despair as his friend was completely withdrawn by what he had just read.

There were a billion questions that had come up in his mind; and he looked for an answer to each and every one of them.

If Pragya's father was factually happy to have met Rohit, why all the boohooing in the first place!

Why was Pragya being cursed by her parents on their having given birth to her?

How could the man who shared laughs with Rohit and his patriarch; suddenly start surviving on medication!

Rohit had never intended to harm anyone, so why were his efforts to unite him and Pragya suddenly an attempt to destroy Pragya's family's integrity?

Pragya had always been Rohit's angel and suddenly he was the one who was playing with her self-respect!

Adarsh permutated and combined several possibilities but simply wasn't able to conclude upon what had actually happened!

He remained still in awe and waited for his buddy who continued to narrate the entire incident:

"A day after I received this mail, her father rang up my dad and told him that I was too tall for his daughter and that we wouldn't look good as a pair. He went on to say that he felt really nice on having met my father and me, however, as marriages are something that are made in heaven and having kept faith in that thought; he didn't feel that the two of us were made for each other."

Adarsh literally jumped off his seat and almost broke the side table that was placed next to his chair:

Holy Crap!

This is ridiculous!

Too tall!

What the hell!

You're kidding right?"

Rohit preserved his vignette and stared at the flooring without uttering a single word.

He seemed tempestuous and his eyes reeked as he kept gazing at the floor without giving away a blink.

The grip that he had on the handle of his chair tightened as he shouted in fury without daring to make an eye contact with his friend:

"Too tall... Huh... Would you believe that Adarsh!

If her father had given me any other damn excuse, which would have seemed to be legit enough, I would've accepted it without raising a single question.

Sacrifice is also a form of love and if sacrifice is what I had to do, I would've done it without oppugning the reasons for my ritual killing. But, this was something that I just couldn't cope with!"

"So, was that it?

"This excuse drove me crazy! I started having this feeling of self-disgust whenever I saw myself in the mirror.

To be true to you, I had never kept an account of my actions while I was with Pragya! Whatever she had asked of me, was served to her without my having any regrets! I never gave a second thought before executing any of her requests because I honestly felt that whatever she had asked for- was for my own good!

But…I seriously hate Facebook! I mean; sure it's a great invention; but it's becoming famous for all the wrong reasons! I hate the fact that people have now started making the virtual world their real world!

I hated it to the core when her mother, without even having met me in real life passed me off as an abuse to mankind!

Then that abysmal request of her to have a glimpse of me in secret without my coming to know about it and Pragya's father denying my proposal on account of my being too tall was something that started making me feel that there was something lacking in me.

And for this very reason bro, I started hating myself. I started hating each and every bit of the virtuoso reality that had been a reason to my being!

I needed an answer to the questions that were coming up in my mind.

Where the hell was I wrong?

I mean, every time the reasons were related to my shortcomings and this was something that I just couldn't live with. I didn't want myself to be a reason for losing my love."

"So…?"

"So, I needed to know the truth!

Yes, it is a known fact that I will be always loved by my parents and will be accepted by them even when I'm at my worst. But, I needed to know what the outside world, especially the girl who had loved me felt; regarding me!

Sometimes I do feel that out of all the forms of love that exist on this planet, it is the love and concern of the blind which is the greatest. It's simply because, they don't fall for the things that lure them. They are free at heart and follow only what they feel is correct and do what their heart tells them to do."

Adarsh *(interrupting)*-"Oh, come on Rohit! You are taking things way too seriously! You are not at all what Pragya's mother proclaims you to be. It's not how you think it is!

And does it actually bother to you what the world thinks of you?

It's pretty obvious that they had certain reasons which they didn't want to disclose and they sought your being tall as an appropriate excuse."

"Today when I think over it, I completely agree to your perception, but, given the situation- I wasn't sane enough to think practically. I really felt that, both Pragya and I should've been given the opportunity to talk ourselves out of everything if things between us did had to come to an end.

But, her mother beheld the fact that if we were to break up, it was better that we didn't talk to each other! So she confiscated her cell phone and locked her up in a room:

After all that has happened, the only question that I ask myself is that- 'hasn't a girl belonging to this generation got the rights to decide to whom to talk and to whom to not to talk to?' I've never forced Pragya into any of her decisions! It was hers for the taking!

"Whoa! Whoa! Whoa! All of this doesn't sound cool enough coming from your mouth.

Where was this intellect of yours when were actually planning to end your life by jumping off from the balcony?"

"I... I do agree that some of my acts are indeed questionable! I am not a saint who'll always be correct! And if you want to accuse me for my wrong doings you're most welcome. Yes, I was extremely wrong in having committed myself to such thoughts!

But now, here I am; my father's true son; having learnt from my mistakes; ready to face anything that comes my way.

Blame me all you can; and I assure you that I shall improve with my blames!

But, what I'm currently trying to get through your head is how girls like Pragya are actually forced to decisions without having a say regarding how they actually interpret the entire situation and what it is, that they actually want to do!

She never even got a chance to complete her education for Christ's sake!

Having born on this planet, I presume that every creature has earned freedom and has the right to express it.

Yes, we can never out do what our parents have done for us, but I really don't think that it is a good idea for us to sacrifice our freedom as an endowment to their deeds.

I mean where the heck was Pragya's mother when we were falling in love?

Why didn't she become the shoulder that Pragya needed when she felt lonely and in need of a friend?

… The reason Adarsh; is coz she can't!

She can never be me and I can never be her!

She can never take my place and neither can I!

Pragya had chosen me in free will; I guess her parents should've been a bit more respectful towards it!

Education, on one hand; brings along freedom and, conservatism; on the other; no matter how stringent it is, should allow these changes to be brought about!

And it wasn't that we hid something! Pragya voluntarily went up to her parents to speak her heart out!

But what's the end result?

Disgust! Hatred! Smuttiness!

And even if according to Pragya's mother, Pragya had done something wrong, shouldn't she be given an opportunity to rectify her acts?

Why did her mother interfere, prohibiting all possible methods to remediate the differences between us?

If we were to be separated, then we could have found our own way.

Weren't we mature enough to do that?

Why the heck did she cease her phone and lock her up in a room?

Adarsh lost comfort in the way he sat as Rohit's canting increased with each elaboration.

He became more cautious as to how he adumbrated himself.

Adarsh's palms turned moist as he stared with deep concern into Rohit's eyes. He remained a silent spectator as Rohit continued with his flamboyance:

"You and I...we belong to the modern world!

We never discriminate women from men! But, the more I have travelled; the more astounded have I found myself to be, only to realize that conservatism still exists in abundance!

People talk of being liberal and very open minded, but, in reality all of that is nothing but lip service.

Most parents to a girl still believe that as soon as their daughters reach their early twenties it is better that they got them married.

Suddenly, their marriage becomes a responsibility which keeps bowing them down with the lapse of time...

It is really a pity that no one has ever spared a thought as to why the minimum age for marriage is 18 amongst girls as compared to 21 for boys in India! And even if it were coz of some biological bullshit; shouldn't girls be given an advantageous position under the educational system under such circumstances?

Things are fucked-up. People take things the way they come to them.

No one questions!

No one gives a damn!

Marriage simply ain't an agreement between two people to spend their lives together. It brings along a lot of responsibilities as well.

I understand that all parents wish to see their children settle down in life, but, shouldn't they be given an opportunity to pursue their dreams?

Is allowing them a couple of years too much to ask for?

Yes, with time, the thought process of many parents has changed but, conservative families still exist in abundance!

When I look around myself, I see so many of my female colleagues not being able to achieve what they actually want to simply because of the social responsibilities they have to meet due to their marriage.

Highly educated 27 year olds are happily marrying off girls who've just reached 20! If they were educated; why didn't they bother to ask their wives if they had any dream that they were willing to live before getting married!

Education my foot!

If anything that people are, they're money minded!

Everyone's a bloody fool!

This sucks man!

But then again, who am I to comment on all this! I have no authority to speak on this subject, yet, I really pity this thought of theirs.

People will continue with their tomfoolery and if I were to ever raise my voice, people would first question me of my position, irrespective of the validity of the questions I raise!"

"You're getting way too philosophical Rohit!

I mean this is how we live!

This is our culture Rohit, which we have inherited over the ages!

We can't change it over night!

Honestly speaking; I wouldn't change all of it.

Women are meant to be the ones who take care of the household stuff.

Doesn't it feel nice when you reach home-all worn out and you have your wife waiting for you!

Wouldn't it feel nice if you were a child and you had your mother at home to take care of you?

Try imagining from a different perspective before giving such dramatic speeches."

"Really Adarsh...?

Hasn't the man of the family got any responsibilities towards his family?

After having been educated in the same school and being taught the same lessons, these are the grounds on which you would like to debate with me?

Dude, I do appreciate ethnicity... But, the only thing that I ask you is with all your views on ethnicity; don't you feel that the woman has been sacrificing a bit too much?

Just because she ain't a man, do her dreams become secondary?

Is it really how you take your stand?

Don't we have the right to raise our voices against what's not correct about our culture?

Are we being educated only to be qualified for our jobs?

All girls aren't princesses and all men aren't monarchs either. But, considering the chances men get to achieve what they want, shouldn't women be given equal opportunities as compared to what a man gets?

And if these inequalities are to exist, then the existence of the dowry system is something which will always prevail in some way or the other.

If that's so, then let's face it Adarsh; that, it is a male dominant society where we live in and all women born in it should start praying the moment they are born into it!

Adarsh-"How...How has all of this got a link with Pragya and you?"

Rohit-"Sure it has!

Rohit paused for a moment in an attempt to search for the correct words to describe his state of affairs.

But, I don't know how I can explain all of what has happened?"

"With words you dumb ass!

You have been blabbering all this while about society! Can you bother to spare a few words for what's actually irritating you?"

"Huh... What's bothering me?

Everything!

Everything that I think of is bothering me!

Sometimes I feel that love marriages are nothing but a dream. The girl can never wait because of the society bullshit and the guy always needs time to settle down!

Does love really exist? I wonder!

I was really hopeful of things once I had met Pragya's father!

And for this reason, I had also made an offering at a nearby temple and couriered it to Pragya.

The reason being that she considered herself to be impure and that she couldn't worship while she was menstruating.

Now tell me; isn't this narrow-mindedness and conservatism personified? How can a girl suddenly be impure just because she's on her periods! And why these taboos...?? Aren't we supposed to have changed! Aren't periods a natural thing!

... Sigh!

Adarsh had been silent for quite a while now! All this while it was Rohit who had been doing the talking! He never rested! Never did he take a moment's pause. The feeling of being a rebel kept flowing through his heart and he kept going on with this normativity:

After she received the courier that I had sent in her name, her mother allowed her to talk to me so that she could thank me... And that was the one last time that I had a conversation with her..."

Adarsh *(in sheer curiosity)*-"...the last time?!"

"Yes, it indeed was the last time that I had had a talk with her ...

Rohit's face turned red with all the talking as he choked in thirst.

A sense of gloom appeared on his face as he went on to elaborate the facts which discomforted his mental soundness.

Her mother never allowed her to talk to me in isolation so; she had to do all the talking while sitting in front of her mother!

Adarsh-"LOL!

There was this very brief moment of laughter that appeared on Adarsh's face following which seriousness crept up his face as it had been prevailing all this while...

Jai ho Conservatism!

Was she able to talk freely?"

"Amidst the hour long conversations that we had, we had decided that if we ever had a daughter in the future, we would be naming her Tamanna - which meant hope!

And after all that had happened, the first question that I asked her on having heard her voice was- 'What about Tamanna?'

She remained silent on this and thanked me for the courier that I had sent in her name!

She continued to say:

'Rohit, you will always be my best friend no matter what happens!

Please do me a last favor by never letting my father know about the mail that I had sent you. It was a mistake...'

I never allowed her to complete her sentence. In fact, I repeated the question that I had earlier put forward to which she then answered:

'Consider whatever you have done for me as what you would've done for your best friend. And it isn't that you haven't had your cup of fun while we were together!'

I was dumb struck when she chose to use the word 'fun' when she had to pick a word to associate my being with her.

Sometimes, people don't intend to speak what they actually want to say and certain words spoken under such a dilemma can be excruciatingly painful.

I was livid when I had heard her use such chinchy words! And out of veering fury I told her that she had used me and if 'fun' is what she associated my being with her, then, her father should definitely know what kind of a daughter he had been soliciting for!

Adarsh *(taking up from where Rohit had ended)-* "You started blackmailing her?

This is so not done Rohit!

And WTF Rohit- 'She used you?'

This was totally uncalled for!

I mean at one place you are accusing her for the words she chose and on the other hand you yourself were using such words!

You never loved her Rohit! You never loved her! I'm guessing the only reason you proposed her in the first place was coz you didn't want to be alone.

Or perhaps she made you feel better about your miserable personal life; but, whatever be it, the truth is that you never loved her...

And I say so, coz even though I don't know much about love but what I do know is that you are never supposed to hurt the ones whom you love.

You simply don't destroy them by their soul if you had loved them!"

"Sometimes, you end up hurting the ones whom you love the most.

I know that what I did was completely wrong, but, in my defense all I can say is that I needed a reason for my denial.

I had to make her succumb in some way or the other, so that she would be forced to make me aware of the reason for my denial.

My self-disgust wasn't allowing me to live freely and this was the very reason I... I pressurized her!"

"Rohit! Rohit! Rohit! This is absolutely not done... You shouldn't have..."

Rohit didn't allow Adarsh to complete what he had to say.

He interrupted him in the middle of his sentence and said:

"I had also forwarded the mail she had sent me, to her sister and marked her CC, so that I could panic her into telling me the reason for my denial."

Adarsh fumed with fury and disgust as he kept staring at Rohit's face.

He was angry yet; he was patient enough and willing to know the reasons behind all that had happened.

He remained a silent spectator, eager to know what his childhood buddy had to tell...

"I am severely incorrect in having done so, but, in my defense all I can say is that I couldn't accept myself as a reason to my not being with her anymore.

After the requests that her mother made and after what her father said, though in a decorous manner; my logical capacity was bamboozled."

Adarsh kept nodding his head as Rohit kept giving excuses.

He wasn't satisfied with his friend's act at this very instant no matter how precise had he been in all his philosophical talks all this while.

"Rohit, she was crying for her father's well-being!

At least spare a thought to that my friend!

...And if there are reasons that can't be spoken of, aren't you mature enough to understand and should you not let things go; rather than hooking yourself to them!"

"It's always easier said than done!

I never wanted to tell anything to her father!

And the reason I scared her with that petty act of mine was because the conservatism that existed in her ménage never allowed me to talk and sort things out.

And spare a thought for me brother; rather than refusing to listen to what I have to say!

I mean how would you feel if someone came and told you that you're no good?

How would you feel if you were referred to, as an abuse to mankind?

"Does it really bother to the Magicman what others think about him?

As far as I know you always proclaimed yourself to be a high-spirited person, then, where were these high spirits of yours when you actually had a chance to simply let things go and achieve greatness in the eyes of the person whom you loved the most?"

Rohit nodded his head in denial.

Adarsh *(continuing)* - "Rohit! Do you have any idea how harsh those words were for a girl of Pragya's stature?

This is so not done!

She begged you for her father's well-being and this is what you did in return!"

"Can I share one more thing with you before you proclaim me as the culprit?"

"Sure…"

"Being a part of the professional world I've learnt the art of using ornamented words, even though I intend to act else ways.

That's something that has been given birth to, by professional hooliganism. And, what I have also learnt is that how one can identify when such words are nothing but ornaments to enshroud the underlying facts!"

"So you mean to say that Pragya…"

"Precisely…"

"Well, how can you be so sure on that?"

Rohit smiled in irony and continued to narrate:

"…because what came next was the actual reason for my denial."

"…And may I know what it was?"

"The actual reason behind my denial was the fact that I was too rich!"

"Too rich…?

Is that actually a valid reason?"

"Believe it or not my friend, it is!"

"...But, isn't that good for Pragya? I don't understand how this is a problem!"

"Pragya's father had the responsibility of getting four of his daughters married and it was necessary for him to think about the society before thinking about anything else."

"This is ridiculous! How has 'what society thinks' got connection to the lives of his daughters?

Shouldn't he..."

Rohit *(Interrupting)* - "A person buttoned down with conservatism simply cannot deny the fact that 'what the society thinks' can be ignored completely.

After all, it is the very same society that he has to live in.

And if the society keeps hitting him with questions every day, life will never be easy!

The society will not like to believe in the fact that he had not given any dowry for the marriage of his eldest daughter and therefore, the problem arises for his remaining daughters!"

"But one simply can't..."

"Adarsh, there's a limit to which a man can resist.

Even goodness has its limits! Somewhere, even the strongest fall.

I mean, I completely agree to what you are trying to explain but, what I'm also trying to explain is that somewhere one can't stand up against conservatism all by himself.

Lest it is a combined effort, even the strongest will falter against the bourgeoisies.

What Pragya's father did was perhaps any conservative father would've done!

And I don't blame him for having done so... He like the many others in this society, are a victim to conservatism and...

...Well; the only grudge that I'll always have in my heart is with Pragya, who not without any specific intention of hers' used a particular word which has hurt me, the most."

"So why don't you call her up and patch up things? Why..."

"Let me tell you another harsh truth about conservatism.

The friendship between a boy and a girl can never remain the way it can between two friends belonging to the same sex so long as there's existence of conservatism in the society.

For the record, we shall always be friends!

But, the truth is that our relation will be nothing but a good social acquaintance.

As children, boys and girls are taught about balance between the sexes, but, unfortunately as we grow up things change. We become 'grown-ups'!

And look at the turn of events!

She hates me for my act!

I'm happy she feels so!

It'll be much easier for her to accept the things that come her way!

At least she can chalk me out as a wrong decision instead of repenting on the fact that we could never be together because of some societal reason!"

"I am not in agreement with your views here Rohit.

Things have changed over the years and things, can now be so different that..."

"Sure it can be... But, it can never be the way it was between Pragya and me!

Pragya and I were best friends... And even if I patch up with her, the truth is that we can never be best buds ever again.

Perhaps a few more years, but certainly not after that!

Perhaps we could still remain friends but, the truth is that, after the things we have shared as best buds, we would be faking our relation so that we could be in touch with each other.

All thanks to conservatism..."

"I still don't agree to what you're saying right now! I mean... It's you and Pragya, god damn it!

Doesn't it bother you to know if she's happy or not?

Aren't you concerned one bit if she's in need of any help or...?"

"I never told you that I've forgotten her bro...

She was, is and shall always be my angel...

I can never forget her... Not even for a single moment in my life.

Yes, I still love her and I will miss talking to her but you're wrong if you think that the joy of life comes principally from human relationships.

An angel sent by the gods is always around us!

It is in everything and in anything that we experience.

People just need to change the way they look at things...

From a distance, if not close enough, I will always be Pragya's angel and will always keep a watch over her life without her getting to know about it.

Whenever there's a moment where she needs help; be rest assured that the Magicman will be there for her..."

"So, what happened to her after all this? Is..."

Rohit kept smiling as Adarsh continued to question him.

Meanwhile, Karan entered the balcony shouting and breaking the silence that had begun to creep up....

"Yo! Yo! Yo!

Where the hell had you guys disappeared last night?

I kept looking for the two of you the entire night but couldn't find you guys anywhere.

And what the heck were the two of you murmuring about?

Were you two doped?"

Rohit and Adarsh kept staring at each other not knowing what to say...

Karan (*continuing*) – "Hey, you know what- I caught a glimpse of Pragya this morning...

She was looking gorgeous in a saree!

Piyush is really lucky to have her in his life."

Rohit-"Absolutely...!

Nothing can match a woman in a saree... Especially Pragya!

(*Smiling*) You know- if I were ever married, I would tell my wife to learn how to flaunt beauty with grace from Pragya..."

Karan-"Hmm... That reminds me of something!

You had a story to tell, didn't you?

What was it all about?

Who is the mystery girl in your life?

Rohit quickly pounced on from where Karan had stopped and started laughing...

"....Hahaha!

I'm certainly a very good story teller. All of that was nothing...

I'm happy being single as of now. Enjoying this small vacation that life has gifted me with... Enjoying my happy holiday!

Happy Holidays!

Love is magic...
Yet magic is sometimes nothing
but a strange illusion!
Love is a manifestation of dreams...
Yet dreams are sometimes nothing
but an unanswered confusion
So much so as the water is to its ocean
Such is the way love binds the
heart in its emotions

Love is an enigma...
And some enigmas are lost
without a profound solution
Love is sometimes a mystery...
And sometimes mysteries can
be a bewitched contusion
Like two people grandeur each
other with sheer devotion
Million bits of mirth cast in a
heartthrob convention

Love doesn't know the rich...
Nor does it recognize any destitution!
Spell bounded and crocheted in fascination
Love indeed is magic...
Yet, magic is sometimes nothing
but a strange illusion!

Chapter 6

The Oddment

"When people hear the word sacrifice; they often associate it with losing something that they love the most.

But, this isn't true at all.

Sacrifice doesn't actually mean losing something for a reason. As a matter of fact; the word – sacrifice; in its crudest sense means giving up something that we love the most; or living with something that we can't live without! Sacrifice is never impelled upon a person. It flows to those vested with free will and courage driven by a settled mind.

Sacrifice, however can never do away with the pain.

The pain will always linger in the hearts of those who make the sacrifice. But, even that pain seems like a specter of facticity when the heart cleanses itself from all ruefulness.

Sacrifice brings pain, but it also brings peace to the heart.

Sacrifice deprives comfort, but it also brings about generosity.

It all depends on how we perceive our sacrifices...

In the end, it all depends on how pure is our love!"

Prateek Surana

"All the wonders of the world I
knew of are gone for sure!
All the wonders that I want; I found in her!
Her world becomes a part of me
As I get mazed to search myself
...And no claims return!

My intuition fails to find its way
I keep searching to mend my ways
Tables turn to question my name
Finding myself more lost
when she's not around
Losing my control; that I wish to find again

Give me a sip of my taste!
Make me drink my own blood
at its purest chaste
I search for my thirst hereafter
Quench it with the drug I'm now after

Everything that I seek; I found in her
All that I need; I found in her
My thirst remains arid
Making me feel more lost than ever again

Every drop of perspiration goes in exile
The closer I reach
The harder it becomes
Few steps to vanquish my chastity
And turn into what I had
chosen to become...

I find myself more lost when
she's not around
Losing my control; when I
find herself in me again
The heart rekindles those forgotten days
...Now remembered by me
as my happy holiday!"

*"...and always remember! It's never the end...
It's always the start to a new beginning."*

Acknowledgements

"Happy holidays" is my expression on the conservatism and double standards that still exists in the modern day society. I firmly believe that the world still has a long way to go before it attains feminism. It still needs to evolve far more than what it already has; before both- men and women are seen as equals.

The many people that I've met and the many stories that I've heard have somewhere compelled me to narrate a story which highlights the ways I feel a woman is being discriminated from a man.

This attempt, however, would have never been possible without the help of a few important people who have guided me and backed me whenever I was a bit dubious.

To my mom and dad, for being the two stanchions of my life! For you, words shall always be insufficient to express my gratitude.

To my Alma Mater, Calcutta Boys' School, for making me who I am!

To Mr. Raja McGee, my principal, for when I had passed out from school, for always having faith in me and entrusting me with responsibilities, I myself hadn't thought I'd be capable of.

To my teachers, Mrs. P Shivdas, Mrs. B.Gupta, Mr. A Bhowmick, Mrs. M. Banerjee, and the entire teaching faculty of Calcutta Boys' School.

To my friends, Priyanka and Shradha, for helping me with your views, which I very badly needed to sketch Pragya's character.

And Ms. Rooposhree Ganguly, for your unconditional support and guidance!